THE SCRYING GAME

CHRISTINE ZANE THOMAS

D1194443

For Tom Garner, Couch—an amazing father, father-in-law,
grandfather, and friend.
Your support meant the world.
Your memory sails on the ocean of our hearts.

"A marriage is always made up of two people who are prepared to swear that only the other one snores."
   - Sir Terry Pratchett

PROLOGUE

I had the dream again...

The dream where the barrel of a gun takes up most of my vision. Two hands crowd the remainder of the space, fingers interlocking. Her red fingernail polish is fresh. Her hands shake like she doesn't know what she's doing. At this range, it won't matter.

I'm done for.

The woman's finger wavers beside the trigger.

My heart hammers fast in my chest. In the dream. In reality. It doesn't matter.

The center of my vision blurs, and the red fingernails are now all I can see.

Her finger slips behind the guard and across the trigger. She squeezes.

BAM!

I WOKE COVERED in sweat with my heart beating just as fast as it had in the dream.

When I was younger, I had the dream too many times to count.

I always woke up.

This was the first time I'd had the dream in a long time. Years.

And like back then, I was still alive because this was a dream—a vision—and that's how visions work. Or at least how my visions worked. They weren't real, but they *always* became a reality.

Well, not always.

Sometimes I'd do something to stop them.

But that was when I was given clues—given solid facts. When I could see who was holding the gun. And given enough context to know why.

This dream wasn't something I could run from. It was a vision. There was no hiding from it. No escape. There was only the knowledge—the *knowing* that one day I would be staring down the barrel of that gun.

1

It was still dark outside the Holiday Inn Express. The lights in the parking lot were bright, shining through a crack between the shades. I couldn't get it to close before bed and finally just gave up. I had turned my back to it, but sometime in the night, I rolled over. The lights were taunting me now.

So was the hotel's alarm clock. It read 5:00 a.m.

The elevator outside my room dinged. Then it dinged again. Sleep is always an elusive thing, but even more so in a hotel. The way these places were set up, I wondered if they were really meant for sleeping or if they were just a cruel joke.

I crawled out of the sheets and showered. I got dressed and spent a few minutes trying to straighten my hair. It wasn't worth the trouble or the time. I slapped on a head-band and contemplated wearing braids again. Then I hit the continental breakfast buffet. I took a box of Fruit Loops and some weak but scalding-hot coffee and got on the road.

The sun had yet to rise.

Six hours of driving later and I'd failed to get the dream off my mind.

It shouldn't have surprised me. The closer I got to my hometown, Mossy Pointe, Florida, the closer I was to confronting my past—and that unavoidable future.

Since I was seven years old, just a child, I'd dealt with visions. This one and others. Many others.

Of all the visions, this was the only one I ever had at night—as a dream.

The others appear in different ways. Usually, when I'm doing something important.

I go rigid. My eyes glaze over; I'm told they're milky white. And there I stay until the vision plays out.

I hated my visions. I hated them so much. For a while, when I was young and stupid, I even blamed my daddy for them. Maybe because the second vision I ever had was of his cancer diagnosis. Or maybe because they came from his side of the family. His aunt was a psychic. A seer. And on top of that, a hundred percent looney tunes.

I got some gas, a Coke, and a snack and put another hour of interstate behind me. In that hour, the world evolved into something familiar. Pine trees as far as the eye could see. The billboards looked like they hadn't changed in twenty plus years. They still advertised local restaurants and Jesus.

My 2003 Honda Civic turned off the interstate on autopilot, as if the tires knew where to go.

Highway 83 was more of the same. The same old man in the same old Ford pickup sold the same old Tupelo honey. He had fresh boiled peanuts and homemade preserves lining the bed of his truck. He waved at me from his lawn chair underneath a big yellow umbrella.

That man would wave to anyone, whether he knew them or not.

He knew me though, Willow Brown. Or he did when I was younger. If he recognized me, he'd be kind enough not to mention the touch of gray in my short, curly black hair or that my hips had filled out. I was still on the short side and more muscular than most women, visible in my arms and lower body. My workouts consisted of pull-ups, push-ups, and heavy squats, not Pilates.

I doubted Mr. Thomas's eyesight was as stellar as it used to be—back when he could see anyone going to and from the interstate and tell their mommas about it.

There never was much to do in Mossy Pointe. Not much trouble to get into. And when I lived here, that was where I liked to be—with the trouble. At least that's what my momma thought.

The town itself is hardly worth mentioning, either on a map or in conversation. Some might go as far as to call it a speed trap—a mile and a half of Highway 83 where the official designation is changed to Main Street and the speed limit drops from fifty-five to twenty-five miles per hour.

My Aunt Cora's house sat at the very end of Main Street. 2002 was the last address before the speed limit bumped back up to fifty-five. After that, there were miles and miles of forest mixed with swampland until the road neared the coast.

The house was a Victorian with a turret above the sitting room, where Cora did her readings. In the window, there was an unlit neon sign with a palm on it. It matched the sign in the front yard.

Madam Cora's Palmistry and Fortunes: Psychic Readings, Tarot Cards, and Consultation.

When the sign in the window was lit, the psychic was available for readings.

I'd grown up in this house with Aunt Cora doing readings daily.

She'd taken us in—me, my mother, my little sister Nora, and my father, just before he died. He'd left us with massive medical bills and giant-sized holes in our hearts.

We all loved Daddy in our own ways. Momma loved his cooking. Nora loved his jokes. And I had to be the daddy's girl. I loved everything about my daddy.

We stayed here until I was a senior in high school, when Momma finally paid those bills off and got on her feet again.

She found a new job in Richmond, Virginia.

My momma had always wanted to leave this place. She used to say people get rooted here, and they can never dig themselves out. She did though. It took her nearly a decade to do it, but she dug the three of us out.

After college, Nora took a page out of Momma's book. She ventured to the west coast, to Seattle. A few years later, Momma followed her there. She moved to a retirement community down the street from Nora and her grandbabies —my niece and nephew.

Since leaving, we hardly ever talked about Mossy Pointe. Or about Aunt Cora. When she died, we didn't even attend her funeral.

So, it came as quite a shock to the three of us that Cora had left me this place in her will.

My home was still in Virginia, in a little town called Creel Creek.

My husband was still there too. But that was a whole other issue.

I had one job ahead of me: to survey the house, take what I wanted—if anything—and put the thing up for sale.

I could only hope someone would be dumb enough to buy it. From what I remembered, the house needed a lot of work. And my memories were twenty plus years old.

Seeing it, my worst fears were realized. My memory was near perfect. Time hadn't been kind to the old house.

Its purplish-blue paint was chipping. The azaleas lining the wraparound porch had either died or grown out of hand. The roof looked like it might collapse if the wind blew just right.

I let out a big sigh and dropped my things on the porch. I had another problem. The key. I'd forgotten to stop at the lawyer's office to get it.

I trudged back to the car, the Florida heat radiating off my skin. It wasn't even summer. It wasn't even close to summer.

"This is why you make people crazy," I told Florida. "Or it's why crazy people move here."

I squinted, but not because of the sun. Another car had pulled in behind mine. A nice car. A BMW.

A woman sat behind the steering wheel. She waved a manila envelope in one hand, then popped out of the car like she was on springs.

She was a tiny thing. Even shorter than me, and that's saying something. And rail thin—if the same wind that collapsed the roof caught her, it might knock her over, then down the driveway and across the road. When she got closer, all I could see was the beauty mark above her upper lip. Except it was no longer a thing of beauty—not with several long gray hairs sticking out of it.

"You must be Willow," she said, smiling. "I'm Marge Kenner. We talked on the phone."

"Yes, I'm sorry. I meant to stop by when I got here." I felt guilty, making her go out of her way.

"That's all right, dear. I was watching for you."

"You were?" I turned skeptical. "Where were you watching from?"

"The office." She nodded in the direction of town. "We're on the other side of the car wash now."

"Oh." I could just see a brick building on the other side of the car wash down the street. "When did Mr. Green move there?"

"Fifteen years ago, this fall," she said with a note of triumph. "Much better than the old office."

"Wow. You've been with Mr. Green that long?" Artemis Green, Esquire represented Aunt Cora's estate.

"Thirty-eight years this December. Artie only graduated law school the year before that. I've been with him practically his whole career. He often says he wouldn't know what to do without me. And it's true—he doesn't know a lick about computers or copiers or fax machines. Not that we use those much anymore."

"That's impressive." I couldn't think of anything else to say. I wondered why neither of them had retired yet.

Marge handed me the envelope. "I have some things for you to sign—along with the key and a copy of the will."

"Do you want to maybe come inside?"

"Oh, no. I was told never to go onto the premises. Not to set a foot inside it. And I do as I'm told. Artie has always been good to me."

"I'm sure he has." I glanced at her BMW in the driveway.

"You'll be taking it as is. Obviously. There's no money in the will for you. I hope you understand."

"Yes. You mentioned that over the phone." I used the trunk of my Civic as a table and signed her paperwork.

"Let us know if you need anything else." She gave me an

appraising look, and a hint of uneasiness appeared in her blue eyes.

I felt it too. I didn't want this place.

"Mrs. Kenner," I said. "If I wanted to sell this place, who would I talk to? Is there a good realtor in town?"

"Oh, there's no realtor in Mossy Pointe. Not for years. Not since Hillary Lester retired. There's no market for houses in our area. No buyers, I'm afraid." She inched closer to me, turning conspiratorial. "We do, on occasion, help folks out. There's nothing a power of attorney can't handle."

That surprised me. But I was desperate. "Could Mr. Green do that for me? Could he sell the house?"

"Oh, I'm sure he could. In fact, I already drew up those papers. He thought you might want to sell. Silly me. I forgot them at the office. I should've put them in that envelope with everything else." She shook her head and the gray hairs stayed perfectly in place. "It's no matter. Mr. Hemingway—our postman—will be by later. I'm sure he can drop them off tonight, if that's okay?"

"That's definitely okay!" Again, I was surprised. "Talk about turnaround service. How do you swing that?"

"The trick with him is to have a dog."

"To *have* a dog?"

"Yes. He loves them, but his wife won't let him have one. Poor thing. He carries treats around in his pocket—pets every dog on his route. Throws a ball for mine."

"He never gets chased?"

"Why would he get chased?" she asked, incredulous.

"No reason."

This town was more bizarre than I remembered. A mailman in love with dogs. And no realtor.

Marge studied the house. "I hope the state of things

doesn't surprise you. It's only been a few weeks, but I've seen houses deteriorate in less time."

"I think it was already there," I said.

She smiled halfheartedly. "I'll get you those papers."

Back on the porch, I dug out the key and opened the door wide but didn't go inside. I was startled by a car honking its horn. I turned to find a maroon Crown Victoria speeding by.

I didn't recognize the car. Maybe I knew them—twenty years is both an eternity and the blink of an eye.

I waved to be polite, then carried in my bags.

The inside of the house was dark. With my elbow, I flipped on the first couple of lights and set the bags down at the bottom of the staircase in the foyer. The stairs, like the flooring, were a worn chestnut-colored wood, full of scratches and scuffs. The railing was painted off-white like the walls. It turned at a landing before heading to the second floor, out of sight.

The right side of the foyer was open and spacious. There was a bench on the wall—a waiting area just outside the parlor. Behind the bench, a hallway led to the kitchen.

My heart stuttered inside my chest when a shadow scampered across the hallway from the parlor into the den.

It was just a cat. A large and fluffy cat, gray with black markings.

I sighed my relief. I could deal with a cat.

"Close the door, you're letting out the air conditioning."

I couldn't deal with a voice.

"Hello?"

At first, I thought the cat had spoken, but that wasn't right. A shadow resolved in the hallway to the kitchen.

"I said close the door," she repeated.

That wasn't going to happen. Not until I figured out who

the voice belonged to and what they were doing in Cora's house.

"Can you hear me?" A woman stepped out into the dim light of the foyer.

She wasn't anyone I recognized, but that wasn't what bothered me.

What bothered me was the smile on her face—a smile that said one of three things. She either knew me, she thought she did, or she was a genuine crazy person.

I wasn't sure I wanted to know which it was.

I was about to find out anyway.

2

"You must be Willow," the woman said. "I've heard so much about you."

"Funny, I can't say the same."

The woman came closer, her bare feet soundless on the wooden floor. She stopped at the foot of the staircase.

It was my move. As she'd asked me to do, I closed the door behind me. I wasn't scared, but I wasn't stupid either. I stayed beside the door.

She was a decade younger than me, or more—perhaps in her mid-twenties. She crossed her arms over her chest, still smiling but saying nothing. Her curly bangs protruded from under a fuchsia head wrap, knotted at the top of her head, completely incongruous with her tank top and shorts.

My police training kicked in. I had questions needing answers. "Who are you? May I ask what you're doing here?"

"I'm Ingrid," she said. "Your new roommate."

"My what, now?"

"Technically, I was your Aunt Cora's roommate. But it's your house now, right?"

"Right." I racked my brain for any mention of a roommate, knowing full well Mrs. Kenner had never once mentioned such a thing on the phone. Or just now.

Maybe that's what all the 'as is' stuff was about.

But no. That didn't make sense either. Mr. Green had already drawn up paperwork to help me sell the place.

"You're upset. I can see you're upset. It's my fault."

"No. Not really. Can I ask you something? Does the lawyer know you live here?"

She grimaced. "It was kind of an under the table deal. They always are, aren't they? I was afraid the power was going to go out. But now you're here." She brightened.

This wasn't good.

I wasn't expecting Cora to have a roommate, but it made a certain amount of sense. How else was she paying the bills? Not by doing readings. She hardly ever took money for them. They were done on some sort of barter system.

Ingrid was still smiling. It felt wrong to make nice now only to crush the girl's hopes in the near future.

I had to tell her.

"I'm sorry, Ingrid. I already have plans to sell this place. So, we won't be roommates for long. Just a few days, tops. Maybe I can help you look for a new place?"

Her face fell. "That's okay. I get it. I do. Thanks for the offer."

"Of course," I said.

I peeked into the den and found the large gray cat spread out on an ottoman.

There was also a couch, a couple of chairs, and a coffee table. I was surprised by a flat screen TV that had replaced the mammoth tube television of my youth.

It must've been some reading to get paid with that.

"Is that your cat?" I asked Ingrid.

She shook her head. "Cora's."

Great.

I added it to the list. I had to get rid of a roommate, sell a house, and rehome a ginormous furball.

"I guess I should get the lay of the land." I ventured across the foyer to the parlor. Ingrid followed.

The parlor was as I remembered it. Thick green curtains covered the wide front windows and explained the lack of outside light. The tablecloth on the reading table was made of the same material, trimmed in gold fringe. Four cushioned chairs were arranged around the table—you guessed it, the cushions were made of the ubiquitous green velvet and trimmed in gold. The wallpaper was gold with green pinstripes, just for a change.

A crystal ball—a decoration more than anything—reflected the light from the crystal chandelier. Several tarot decks were stacked haphazardly at the edge of the table, which was strange. Cora stored her decks in a box hidden under the table.

The rest of the room was filled with odds and ends—bookshelves, end tables, tall lamps, and what looked to be a card catalog from a library. These were covered with knick-knacks, candles, and a rainbow assortment of crystals.

A sculpture of a palmistry hand reached up from an end table, ready to grab someone, reminiscent of Thing from *The Addams Family.*

Everything seemed to be in order. A bit dusty but in order. Aunt Cora was all about outward appearances. No one ever saw the disarray that was the upstairs where she hoarded the things given to her as payment—books, clothes, guitars, sacks of potatoes she'd swear were still good. She kept everything.

I wasn't ready to confront that yet, not in my first hour

here. I clicked on some lamps and watched a plume of dust waft about the room, dancing in the light.

"Ingrid," I said. "Can I ask why you were in the dark?"

"It's bright enough out." Her head turned toward the den where the blinds were open. "Plus, it saves on the electric bill. That's always a good thing."

A roommate who cared about the monthly bills. At least Aunt Cora had taught her well.

I followed her gaze to the ottoman where the cat was still lounging. It was watching me.

I went through the hallway to the kitchen, which was about the same as I remembered, and checked for any food left in the refrigerator or the pantry.

Ingrid either didn't eat much or she kept her food in her room. I began a mental list of groceries, and my stomach growled.

The blinds were open and the kitchen was flooded with light.

"Is anything else going to surprise me?" I asked Ingrid. "Probably not."

We were both startled by pounding on the front door. "Who could that be?"

Ingrid shrugged. "I never get visitors." She didn't move to answer the door. She stayed there with her back against the counter, looking out the window at the sun-filled sky.

I guessed it was up to me to find out who was battering the door.

3

Before I could get there, another hand rapped on the door. I could tell because I heard two distinct voices outside, and this knock was lighter than the first. I had my hand on the knob when the first knocker pounded again, as hard as the first time.

It wasn't even locked—they could've waltzed in if they wanted. But that wasn't the way in Mossy Pointe. Doors were typically left unlocked, or they had been in my youth. Doors were respected. They were boundaries meant to be observed. This door especially so. Burst in on a reading and suffer the consequences in your own.

Whoever was on the other side of the door was someone from Mossy Pointe. Probably someone I knew.

Whoever was on the other side was trouble.

I'd been the official owner of the house for less than thirty minutes. And I already regretted it.

I opened the door and shielded my eyes from the sun. The two people on the porch stepped forward.

Scooting aside, not because I wanted to, but because I had to. Otherwise, I would've been barreled over. I allowed them both to brush past me. The first woman went straight for the parlor. The second stopped in the foyer. Her face mere inches from mine, she eyed me up and down, taking my measure.

"Look at you, all grown up and pretty. All I've done is grown out."

"Shawna." I sounded as flustered as I was. "It's good to see you too."

"I knew it'd be you here," Shawna Grimes said. She called into the parlor, "Told you it'd be Willow."

"I didn't disagree, now, did I?" bellowed Alaina King, Shawna's best friend. "It ain't like it's some big secret she was getting this house. The whole town knows."

"Still, it *is* a surprise," Shawna said with emphasis on something being a surprise.

"What is?" My own voice had taken on a tinge of Mossy Pointe twang.

"Turning on the sign," she answered.

She followed Alaina into the parlor, me trailing behind her.

They both looked like they'd come straight from the salon—hair and makeup done, nails manicured.

Shawna wore a knee length skirt and a red top complemented by her matching purse, jewelry, lipstick, and nails. She was freckled and pale with straight red hair and hazel eyes that seemed to change depending on the light.

Alaina wore a romper style dress with sunflowers printed on it. She had a beautiful natural bronzy complexion. Her dark curls were pulled back. She pushed up her hipster sunglasses to reveal her big brown eyes.

She settled into the seat beside Aunt Cora's reading chair.

"What sign?" I asked them, flustered. "What are you two talking about?"

Alaina cocked her head. "You know what sign."

"*The* sign." Shawna looked pointedly back and forth from me to the curtain. "Come on, Willow."

It took me a minute to do the math. The curtain was over the parlor window. The window with the neon palm. And I could see a sliver of red and green light emitting from behind the curtains.

Shawna took a seat on the other side of the reading chair. Then she rested her palm on the table.

"No. No. No." I backed away. "That's not me. I didn't turn on *that* sign."

"You did though. Or someone did." She looked around.

Ingrid hadn't emerged from the kitchen.

Shawna was right. With my elbow, I *had* flipped on both switches beside the door. I'd turned on the foyer light and also told the whole town that the parlor was open for business.

"I didn't mean to turn on that sign." I rushed to the front door and turned it off.

"It's not going to be that easy," Alaina called.

I went back into the parlor and sat down at the table. "Why's that?"

"Cora told us you have the sight."

"She didn't," I said.

"And by us—" Shawna smirked "—she means all of her clients."

Alaina nodded emphatically.

"That's not exactly true." Yes, I had visions, but I didn't have the sight. Not like Aunt Cora.

"Like that's gonna matter to them." Shawna waved, indicating the rest of the town. "Cora's been gone, what, a month now? Two? Folks will be lining up over here. You'll see. It's their routine. They need it."

"You mean the ones who haven't gone elsewhere?" Alaina asked pointedly.

"We're not talking about that right now," Shawna shot back.

"Well, we're not doing that either." I pointed at Shawna's hand.

"Come on, Willow."

I had gotten too close. She thrust her hand my direction, and my reflexes decided to grab it. What I really wanted was to scurry away.

My vision began to cloud over with what else—a vision.

At first, everything was white, a milky fog. Then I was in their salon—their business. I could see Alaina out of the corner of my eye. I was working on someone's hair.

The trill of a telephone shattered the vision. Time passes differently in visions than it does in life—I was probably gone just a second or so. Neither Shawna nor Alaina had noticed.

On the occasional table to my left there was an old rotary telephone, a real vintage collector's item in the same purple color as the house. It looked as fake as the crystal ball, but it couldn't be. It trilled again.

"Good thing this isn't a *real* reading," Shawna said sourly.

"Cora always took it off the hook," Alaina pointed out.

"For one—I never said I'd give you a reading." But seriously, who still has a landline these days? "For two—I didn't know it was there."

"Best answer it," Alaina said. "It's probably someone else who saw the light on. They'll be trying to book the next appointment."

"Then I definitely don't want to answer it."

The phone rang again. I swear it got louder.

They both gave me dirty looks.

"Fine." I picked it up from the cradle. "Madam Cora's Palmistry and Fortunes. This is Willow speaking." The words rolled off my tongue as if it hadn't been twenty plus years since I'd answered a phone in this house.

"You made a mistake coming here," someone said cryptically. A female someone. In the background, I could hear an engine idling.

I let it idle.

"Did you hear me?"

I realized I could hear the same engine with my other ear too.

"Yeah...I did." I got up, stretching the phone cord to the window. I struggled with the curtain, pushing it away, then inched up a blind to see outside.

In the driveway, there were three cars—my Honda, a red Dodge Challenger that either belonged to Shawna or Alaina, and at the road, a Crown Victoria. It was the same car that had honked earlier.

I still didn't recognize it, but I knew that model pretty well. I had driven a Crown Vic for years. And like mine, this car resembled a police interceptor with a grill guard and a spotlight by the driver's side mirror.

Its engine rumbled.

"You might've heard me. But were you listening?" the woman asked.

"You said coming here was a mistake." In theory, I tended to agree with her. But in principle, I wasn't going to say so. "Who are you? What do you want?"

"I'm like you," she answered.

"What do you mean you're like me?"

"I know things I shouldn't. I see the future. I see you in trouble. That is, unless you leave this town. Leave it tonight. Today. You could go now and never look back. After tonight, bad things will play out—and there's nothing you can do to stop them."

"I'm not a fan of threats," I said.

"I don't do threats. I make predictions." She hung up.

Alaina came to the other side of the window. She peered out and said, "Are you kidding me right now?"

"What?" Shawna asked, confused.

"It's Scarlett."

The car reversed into the highway, then barreled up the street.

"Who's Scarlett?"

"Scarlett Myst." Alaina sighed.

I had no clue who or what a Scarlett Myst was. "Is that name supposed to mean something?"

"It's your rival," Shawna said. "The other psychic in town."

"I'm not a psychic. I have no rival. No rivalry. I don't want any of this."

"She's a wannabe," Alaina said. "She's been trying to scoop up Cora's clientele. In fact, she tried to do it before Cora even passed. She runs a parlor out of her townhouse."

"And her name is Scarlett Myst?"

"Stage name. I don't know her real one." Alaina headed back to the table. "I told Shawna it sounds like a stripper name."

"It kinda does," I agreed.

Shawna's face soured. "I think she's all right."

"That's because you've been going to see her."

"Twice." She shrugged. "She's nice—way nicer than Cora ever tried to be. And her prices are reasonable too."

Alaina rolled her eyes, sinking back into a seat. "She's a fraud. You'd see that if you weren't so caught up in your own drama."

"What drama?" I asked.

"Oh, you name it. This one's always worried about something she can't control."

"That's the whole point of this," Shawna argued. "I *can* control it. I control the energies I allow into my life—and the energies I put out." She crossed her arms, defiant.

"Is that why y'all are here? To control your energies?"

"No." Alaina shook her head. "We're here because of what happened to Beau yesterday. You remember my brother Beau, right?"

She was teasing but her question was serious. I wanted to roll my eyes anyway.

Shawna—in on the joke—playfully slapped Alaina's shoulder. "Of course she remembers Beau. They were best friends up until high school."

"That's right. I remember." Alaina stroked her chin. "What'd he do to you? Why'd y'all fall out?"

I had never told them why. Twenty years was long enough ago to confess. "He kissed me."

"He did? What, now? And you didn't want him to?"

"Worse." Time for the real truth bomb. "I did."

"Oh." They were both taken aback. Their joke wasn't funny anymore. Not that it was to begin with.

"I didn't know you liked him like that."

"Me either," Shawna said.

"Yeah, well, neither did he." I leaned against the wall, staying well away from the reading table.

Shawna and Alaina, plus Alaina's brother Beau, made up half of the group I hung out with growing up. That's what we called it in the Nineties—hanging out.

Like a typical teen, I fell in love with my good friend's brother.

He had kissed me on a dare, then proceeded to pretend it was the grossest thing he'd ever experienced. That day, my heart broke into a million pieces.

"No big loss." Alaina tried to cheer me up. "Beau's an idiot anyway. You're better off."

"And I heard you're married," Shawna said.

"What's marriage got to do with an ex-crush?" Alaina scowled. "So what. If I was married, I'd still pine after every ex that got away."

Shawna was horrified. "Why?"

"Because they got away," Alaina replied. "But I'm mostly talking about James Marsden."

"James Marsden didn't get away from you." Shawna laughed. "Granted, if he saw you, he'd sure try."

I had to laugh too. "I'm glad some things never change. Y'all are as hilarious as ever. And yes. I'm married."

"Okay. Where is this mystery man from Virginia?"

"Still in Virginia. At our house. Where we live."

"Uh huh." Her brow furrowed. "He didn't want to come down? Let me guess—he couldn't get the time off."

"Something like that."

They exchanged a look and closed their mouths. There was a lot more to this story, but it wasn't something I was ready to spill. Not to them—especially not after they'd ambushed me.

"So, what happened to him?" I asked. "What's going on with Beau?"

"You remember Perry Robinson?"

I nodded.

"You heard he got murdered, then?" Alaina asked.

I hadn't.

"It *was* unsolved." Shawna inclined her head. "At least until yesterday."

"They arrested Beau." Alaina stared at the table and set her own forearm down beside Shawna's. "We thought maybe you could give us a read on it."

"That's not what I do." I shook my head. "And neither of your palms will help Beau. But you can tell me more about what happened to Perry."

I remembered Perry Robinson as a lanky little kid who followed our group everywhere until Beau capitulated and let him into the group. The last I knew, he and Beau were close friends—not exactly the type to go killing each other.

"He was shot," Shawna said. "That's all we know."

"When?"

"About six month ago," Alaina said. "Maybe seven?"

"Seven," Shawna agreed.

"And they just made an arrest?"

Shawna nodded.

Alaina's eyes widened. "It wasn't Beau. You know that."

"I don't know anything," I said. "I haven't talked to either of you in how many years? I haven't seen Beau in more than twenty. Things change. People do too."

"They don't change that much," Alaina said. "They don't become killers. You know my brother. You know me. Give me a reading and I'll show you."

Unfortunately, she was wrong. It didn't matter whether people changed or not. Anybody can make a mistake. Or a rash decision. For all I knew, Beau did kill Perry.

"I already told you I don't do that."

"Your aunt said you have the gift. She said that's why she was leaving this place to you."

"Yeah. Didn't she ever teach you anything?" Shawna asked.

"Never."

"You've seen readings though. You've seen 'em done a thousand times. Some of that had to rub off."

This was true. I'd seen hundreds of readings over the years. But seeing my aunt tell someone their fortune and knowing how she did it—those were very different things.

Psychic reading isn't an exact science, and my visions weren't something I had control over. When I touched someone, about half the time I saw something. It was problematic, and I tried to avoid touching people—who wants some stranger offering random advice out of nowhere?

A reading is different. Generally, the client seeks the answer to a question and the psychic finds the answer and shares it with the seeker. Not me. If someone asked me about their love life, all I'd be able to tell them would be that they were going grocery shopping or getting a new vacuum. My visions were frequently nonsensical, at least to me.

"Plenty of cards around here." Shawna picked up a tarot deck. "How hard is it to shuffle and lay a few out?"

"You'd still want me to interpret them."

"What if you just show 'em to me? No interpretation needed. And free of charge, of course. I've seen this deck before. I know how they read."

"Forget cards." Alaina plopped her hand down again. "Come on, Willow. Try a reading. It's not hard."

"I am *not* touching your hand," I said firmly.

For the first time since she'd arrived, Alaina showed me how she really felt about Beau's arrest. A tear streaked down her cheek.

Dadgummit. Her face.

I snatched the tarot deck away from Shawna. Only I wasn't careful enough. When I did, my fingers grazed her pinky. It was the briefest of contact, but it was enough.

I saw Shawna tripping down the porch steps on her way out.

The vision happened so fast, there was no way they noticed my eyes glaze over.

"Here we go." I shuffled and gave the cards to Alaina to cut, then dealt out two cards on the table. They were both inverted. "There you go. Now, get out. I don't have time for any more of your foolishness."

"What about Beau?" Alaina asked.

"What about him?"

"You're gonna help us, aren't you?"

"I wouldn't know where to start." That was a boldfaced lie.

"Start with the police," Alaina said. "The city and the county. They aren't like they were in the old days. You know Josh is a deputy?"

I did know that. Josh was my second cousin and Aunt Cora's grandson. How he hadn't inherited this place was beyond me.

I ushered the ladies to the front door.

"Goodbye. It was nice seeing you. Oh, and Shawna, watch that step there." She maneuvered around the tripping hazard.

I closed the door and let out a huge sigh.

What have I gotten myself into?

For a second, I thought about taking Scarlett Myst's advice, picking up my keys and cruising out of town as fast as I'd come.

Except I hated threats more than any ghost from my past.

I wondered where Ingrid had disappeared to—if she went to her room upstairs or if she was still in the kitchen.

Had she been listening?

Down the hall, the cat popped its head out of the den. I'd forgotten about it.

"Those were some lies you told."

I knew that voice. I knew it well.

No matter what I thought I heard, it had to be my ears that were liars because that voice belonged to Aunt Cora.

4

The cat plopped down on its haunches. With a smooshed face and scruffy hair, it looked anything but regal. As if sensing my opinion, it puffed out its chest and stared back at me through calculating yellow eyes, its tail twitching.

I'd never been a cat person. They scared me when I was young, more so than dogs. Sharp teeth, sharp claws—even a playful cat left me with scratched up arms and legs. What I hated most about cats was their hair trigger—how they flipped a switch, going from playful and friendly to something else entirely. Dogs have never heard of too many belly rubs. Pet a cat for a second longer than they want you to and pay the price.

I squatted and said, "Come here, kitty."

It didn't move. I leaned closer to stroke the cat's fluffy back, and it obliged by leaning into my hand.

Finally, I was able to relax. I sighed and let go of my fears —including the anxiety that led to my hearing Aunt Cora's voice in the hallway. It was the stress talking. Literally talking, in my Aunt Cora's voice.

The idea that I was hearing things wasn't great. But it was better than the alternatives: wondering if Ingrid was a talented ventriloquist who could not only mimic my great aunt's voice to a T but could throw it several rooms away.

Or the other alternative—my aunt lingering as a ghost.

I shivered.

The cat sensed my mood and stiffened. Wary, I gave her one last stroke. "Now, that wasn't so bad, was it?"

She stretched with a little moan.

I smiled and joked, "You know, for a second there, I thought you said something."

"I did say something." The voice was louder and definitely coming from the area of the cat—whose mouth hadn't moved.

It was times like these I hated being psychic the most. Aunt Cora's ghost had to be here, haunting me. Or worse than that—she wasn't actually dead.

And yes, I know how that sounds.

I'd seen ghosts before. They passed me on the street or quite often, in a hotel room—like the one I'd stayed in the previous night.

But their ghostly eyes hardly ever lingered on me. As a general rule, ghosts are not concerned with the living world or the people in it.

I saw no ghost in this room. Just an ugly cat.

My mind slowly came to grips with the situation. "Aunt Cora, is that you?"

"It took you long enough," she said. "You took the scenic route. And I'm not just talking about the house. That too. Why'd it take you a month to get here? You know, you used to be my favorite."

"I had some things at home." It wasn't really a subject I wanted to talk about. I got to the point. "How are you a cat?"

"That's neither here nor there. Why did you tell those girls so many lies?"

"Those weren't girls. We're nearly forty. And they weren't lies. Not exactly." I averted my eyes from the yellow cat eyes currently penetrating my soul. "You never taught me any of those things."

"It wasn't for lack of trying," Aunt Cora argued. "You ran off every time I did. You wouldn't face your abilities head-on and now look at you. Can't read a palm. Can't shuffle cards."

"I don't want to read palms. I never asked for this gift."

"You know as well as I, it's not a gift. But that doesn't mean you shouldn't use your abilities. There's plenty of good that comes with them, along with the bad. You could've helped those girls. You could help your old boyfriend."

"He was never my boyfriend. And he's not my friend. Not anymore."

"You can't say you aren't curious about what's going on."

"Of course I'm curious. I work in law enforcement. But it's not my case or any of my business."

I stood up, and it slanted the conversation from bizarre to slightly comical. I was talking to a cat. What would Ingrid think? Or did she know?

Oddly, this felt more like an ambush than the actual ambush by Alaina and Shawna. At least they'd knocked on the door when they'd seen an opportunity. Aunt Cora had lain in wait. This whole thing—inheriting her house—was a trap.

"You should call your cousin and find out," Aunt Cora said.

"Yeah, I'll get right on that."

"You will?"

"No." I rolled my eyes. "Why are you so interested? And why are you a cat?"

"It's complicated."

"Which part?"

"The cat part," she said and continued, "I'm interested because those two girls—"

"Women."

"Those two women weren't telling you the whole story."

"To be fair to them, I wasn't asking many questions. Now, why are you a cat?"

"You aren't going to let it go, are you?"

I shook my head.

"You're the reason I'm a cat." The words came out like the accusation they were. "I made a promise to your father. He left it up to me to train you. And I let you run off when you needed me the most. I always held out some hope you'd come back."

"I almost did. A few times." Her words had struck a chord. Bringing up my father—that was a low blow. "Did Daddy really ask you to teach me?"

"You think I'd skip the afterlife for anything less?"

"Probably not." This really was a trap.

"Are you going to listen to me this time?"

"Also, probably not." Slowly, I backed toward the front door.

"Where are you going?" The cat sprang up in an attempt to follow me. And I slammed the door between us before she could escape.

From the porch, I yelled, "I'm going to get something to eat." Quieter and to myself, I said, "And I'm going to reevaluate my whole life."

5

L eaving the Honda in the driveway, I set off toward town at a brisk pace. The shade from the pines gave some reprieve from the heat. The sun was setting.

I walked down the road for several hundred feet before reaching the sidewalk that ran through most of town. It was broken and cracked with weeds and roots growing up through it.

The road was in better condition—the difference between being maintained by the city versus the state or county.

Creel Creek had similar problems. It always seemed like the city's funds were diverted to projects that only a select few people cared about. The problem being those select few were filling the mayor's pockets.

And Creel Creek was larger than Mossy Pointe. Much larger. Barely a thousand people called Mossy Pointe home. And that was counting those who lived outside the city limits but within the post office boundary.

My stomach growled as I passed the high school. I got a

better look at Artemis Green's new—or new to me—law office. It was a two-story brick building, standing well above the car wash next to it. There were narrow floor to ceiling windows around the whole of the second story. They probably had the best view of town, looking out in all directions.

That's how she saw me. But how'd she know it was me?

I got an answer a few seconds later. A car sped by, flying from the interstate toward the coast.

On my way into town, I had slowed down to the speed limit. An unfamiliar car obeying the law. I stood out. Plus, from her vantage, she might've seen me turn into Cora's driveway.

I crossed the road there, mindful of speeding vehicles. It was just another block to my destination.

Sabal's Grill and the Majesty Diner were staples of the Mossy Pointe food scene. Competing diners, directly across the road from each other. Other restaurants came and went —mostly, they went. All except the Italian restaurant on the other side of town. Oddly, it served the best fish sandwich.

For several reasons, my heart and my stomach were set on Sabal's Grill. It was the reason I'd foregone a fast-food lunch.

All the buildings on this block shared a common wall but had individual facades. Sabal's Grill was on the end. Its name was painted on the plate glass window. A placard in the window read OPEN, but it was almost time for the break between lunch service and dinner. *? at sunset ?*

I was cutting it close, but I'd planned it that way.

A bell jingled, announcing my arrival.

Nikki Mitchell, née Gregg, stood a head taller than me. She wore a warm wide smile, her teeth too white and too many to count. She had big brown eyes and eyelashes to envy.

Since the second grade, when we hit it off immediately, we'd been the best of friends. We'd gone to the same university, pledged the same sorority, and graduated together. I was the maid of honor at her wedding. She was the matron of honor in mine.

We shared everything with each other. Almost everything.

Nikki didn't know about me. Or rather, she didn't believe psychics were real. I tried not to give her—or anyone, for that matter—a reason to think otherwise.

"Aren't you a sight for sore eyes?" Nikki dimpled. "Look at you, girl." She called over her shoulder, "Henry, look at my bestie. She gets better with age. She's like a fine wine."

"She is," Henry, her handsome husband, agreed. He aged like a vampire—I'd know. He looked just like he did in their wedding photos, minus the tuxedo.

He carried a tray of dishes over from an empty table. "And you, my dear, are the most expensive Scotch."

"Are you saying I'm expensive?" she asked.

He chuckled. "I'm saying I'm a lucky man."

"You're both sweet talkers." I scooted around the counter and wrapped Nikki in a hug. "It's so good to see you."

"You too. Ouch. I still have ribs under these curves."

"Sorry."

"It's been, what, five years, now?" she asked. "We did that girls' weekend in Vegas. Whatever happened to 'we're going to do this every year from now on?'"

Henry leaned in for his own hug. "Finances happened. We had that down year. Plus, that other thing."

Nikki shook her head. "I told you. I won't gamble next time."

"And I told you it's a sin to lie to your husband."

"It's actually just the lying that's a sin," I interjected.

"Then this girl needs to head to church ASAP." He smirked. "That's as soon as possible, Nikki Mitchell. I'll bring that classic car of yours around right now."

"Is she still driving that Mustang?" I asked him.

"She's a classic," Nikki said.

Henry rolled his eyes for my benefit. "The classic era of the Mustang ended well before the Fox body. Am I right?"

"Five-point slow." We bumped knuckles.

Nikki glared at us. "Say what you will about my house, my restaurant, or my rotten kids. But leave Foxy alone."

"Oh. I'll leave her alone," he said. "It's the reason I drive my truck up here before you're even up in the morning. Foxy smells like mold and bad decisions."

"If I recall, some of those bad decisions were yours."

Henry gasped. "How dare you call my children bad decisions? Misguided decisions, maybe. But not bad."

"I don't know how we ever fit in that backseat."

"I don't want to think about it," Henry said.

I raised my hand. "Uh, neither do I."

Nikki laughed and took me by the hand. "The real reason we drive separate cars is I have to get those rotten kids to school. I believe I deserve that extra hour of sleep."

"Uh huh," Henry grunted.

"I've got an idea," Nikki said to him. "You can get in that kitchen and cook my bestie whatever she wants. We've got some catching up to do." She dragged me away from the counter.

"That I'll do." He grinned. "It's nice seeing you, Willow. Don't be a stranger. We're here seven days a week."

Henry pushed through the double doors to the kitchen.

"Seven?" I whispered. "You're open Sunday?"

She nodded. "We have to be—or so that man claims.

Everything's a competition. At least it is when it comes to Majesty over there. They did it first."

"Because of course they did." I shook my head. "I don't understand why Henry cares so much. When we were kids, he swore he'd never work here. Now you two practically live here."

"He's got to carry on his daddy's fight. And his daddy's recipes. I just have to let him do." We took a corner booth. "I'm glad you came at our slow time. In an hour or so, this place will be filled with people, and there'll be a line outside by the benches."

"Seriously?"

"Hence the reason I let him run the show. He's doing something right. That, and I swear no one wants to cook at home anymore. At least not every night."

"I don't blame 'em. I hate dishes. Come to think of it, cooking too."

She laughed. "You and me both. There's a reason I work the front of the house."

A waitress I didn't recognize brought me water and a menu. I didn't need either. "I'll take a Coke and a bacon cheeseburger with fries."

"Some things never change."

"What? You expect me to order a salad?"

She rolled her eyes, then lifted her chin to the waitress. "I'll have my usual."

"What's your usual?"

Nikki pointed at a picture of a chicken Caesar salad. "I just want to know how you eat the way you do and keep so trim."

"I work out," I replied. "Plus, I haven't eaten much of anything today. Just road snacks. Chips and a candy bar."

"I gain five pounds if I *look* at road snacks." She narrowed her eyes. "Don't you laugh. It's true!"

I laughed.

What I loved most about being with Nikki was how easy our conversations came. We could go weeks without talking to each other, and with a text or a phone call, pick right up in the middle of a conversation.

Of course, there were some conversations I preferred not to pick up again.

"I notice you're by yourself..."

"I told you I would be."

She sighed. "I was hoping you were wrong. How's Tim doing?"

"Do we have to do this?" I sipped my Coke. "We've been over this."

"Maybe things changed."

"They haven't. I didn't even call him last night."

"Willow!"

"It's not like he called me."

"Still."

"Can I please enjoy my burger in a Tim-free zone?"

"You already are. He isn't here."

"You know what I mean."

She frowned. "Fine. I'll pretend to enjoy this salad in this zone with my best friend."

"You wouldn't've enjoyed it anyway."

"True. But I'd enjoy the company more if she weren't in a mood."

"You put me in this mood. What are you going to do to fix it?"

The edges of her lips turned up, just slightly. "You're evil."

"That's not new."

"I'm eating a salad."

"You deserve a medal, not to mention a dessert."

"Ice cream sundaes?"

"Obviously."

"Be right back."

When Nikki returned with our ice cream, I told her about the drive down and filled her in on the pertinent details of the house, including Ingrid and the cat but leaving out that it was talking with Cora's voice.

"I've seen that cat," she said. "A few months ago, before Cora passed. It was stalking something in the front yard, its big old belly grazing the ground. That thing has to weigh thirty pounds."

"Probably."

She licked her spoon. "I wouldn't want to live in the same house with something like that. What if it tries to smother you in the middle of the night?"

"Then I'll go quietly." I smiled.

"You're welcome to stay with us. The kids could share a bed for a few nights."

"No. I don't want to put you out."

"You know it wouldn't. The kids would love to see you."

"I'd love to see them. I *will* see them. But I don't have to stay there, and I've got too much to do at Cora's."

"Like turning on that light?"

"An accident. Who told you?"

She scanned the now empty restaurant. Henry was humming in the kitchen. A waitress counted her tips on a table across the room, and the dishwasher had already come by, sweeping up before the dinner crowd.

Nikki lowered her voice anyway. "Marcy Chase was driving by and saw it on. She was on her way to get her nails done. She told Alaina and Shawna while she was there."

"That's how they knew," I said. "I was wondering how they saw from the salon."

"They're the tip of the iceberg. After her nails, Marcy came right over here and had lunch with a few other gals. I overheard her telling them about it. I'd wager by now, the whole town knows that sign was on. We don't even need social media. Although, I bet it's on there too."

"Great. I didn't think anyone here knew how to use the internet."

"Oh, they do," she said. "Someone even made a group to chat about Perry's murder. All anonymous and stuff. But no one had been on it in months. Not until yesterday. Then it blew up."

"I know about Beau. That's why they wanted their fortunes read."

"If anyone needs their fortune read, it's Beau."

"Do you think he did it?" I asked her.

She shrugged. "I've heard lots of rumors. About Beau. About Perry. But honestly, Willow, it's not like I know either of them anymore. A town as small as this one, and I've kept in better touch with you."

"I understand that."

I asked about the happenings in Mossy Pointe over the past few years—the past year in particular. It sounded like a whole lot of nothing.

But, I thought, *that's how it always is in a small town.* Looks could be deceiving, and there was a lot going on beneath the surface.

To get the whole picture, I needed to ask the right question.

6

By the time we were done catching up, there was barely a hint of golden orange light remaining in the sky. It was already dark outside, and I'd yet to survey the upstairs rooms of Cora's house.

I didn't know if there was a bed for me to sleep in—or a bed I'd want to sleep in. Maybe I'd have to take Nikki up on her offer.

The closest name brand hotel was almost an hour away. While the Mossy Pointe Inn had always put out Norman Bates vibes, it wasn't a psycho killer I'd be worried about. The rumor was they had cockroaches so big they needed their own area code.

I shuddered at the thought of sleeping there.

The walk home was short and uneventful. Or it was until the sidewalk ended and I started to hear voices. Not *those* kinds of voices—not ghosts or urgent messages in my head.

In the dying light, I could just make out a crowd of people outside of Cora's house. There were cars in the driveway and parked on the road. But not everyone had driven. The crowd on the front porch spilling all the way to the sidewalk was proof of that.

The Honda was blocked in. If it hadn't been, I would've devised a plan to sneak into it and make a getaway. That name brand hotel fifty miles away was calling my name.

I stopped at the edge of the property and stewed for a minute. In so many ways, this was a violation. It was a violation of my property, my time, and most of all, my patience.

"Try the door again," a lady on the first step asked of the woman at the door.

"I knocked," the woman countered.

"Knock louder," another yelled.

"Try the handle," the first lady said.

"I'm not doing that." The woman at the door turned to scowl at the suggestion and somehow found me instead. "There she is right now! Willow." She waved. "Don't be shy, now. We're just here to say hello."

Every eye was on me. Dozens of people, mostly women, mostly my age or older. I knew all of them by name.

I gave each person I passed a halfhearted smile. Most didn't return it. Their arms were folded and their lips pressed tight. These ladies didn't appreciate being put out.

On a good day, none of them was what you'd call patient. Right now, they were holding their tongues because they still believed I could offer them something.

I was about to make matters a whole lot worse—mostly for myself.

Not only had I made them wait here after turning on the sign—however briefly—I was about to tell them that they'd waited in vain.

The woman on the steps grabbed my hands, squeezing. "Now, Willow, I was here third. Gladys and Marcy got here before me. But you know Marcy—she's here for the gossip and that's it."

"Not true, Colleen," the frumpy woman ahead of her—Marcy—snapped. "You can wait your turn like the rest of us."

"Easy for you to say. You've only got to wait for Gladys."

I pulled free of Colleen's grasp and reached the top step unscathed. For now.

With my back to the door, I raised both hands to quiet the crowd. They settled down to a few whispers.

"Listen," I said. "I don't know what you've heard." That was a lie. I did know. "But I'm not seeing anyone tonight. I'm not seeing anyone ever. I don't do readings."

"The light was on earlier," someone protested.

"That was an accident."

"I heard you gave a reading," Marcy announced.

"No," I said. "It wasn't a real reading. I pulled a couple of cards. That's it."

"I'd take cards," someone else offered.

"Me too."

I shook my head, my arms still held up like the conductor of the high school band. "I don't think y'all are getting the point. I'm not here for this. Madam Cora's isn't open. I'm sorry."

I wasn't sorry.

There was a low murmur of complaints.

"Listen. It's my first night here. I have to unpack. I have to settle in. Y'all understand where I'm coming from, right?"

"Then, when will you be open?" Gladys asked. "You can book me the first appointment."

"I told you, I won't be."

This wasn't to their liking.

Colleen was of the opinion that I was full of another

word for horse excrement. Things were said that couldn't be taken back. More than one told me I was squandering my gift, others doubted I had it. Gladys said she was disappointed in me, and weirdly that hurt me the most.

Weirder still, Marcy went away with a smile on her face as if the commotion she'd egged on was exactly what she really wanted.

They finally quieted enough for me to say, "I'm sorry," but I doubted any of them believed it.

I opened the door and ducked inside, driving the bolt home for good measure.

For a long while, I stayed there, resting the back of my head on the door. After ten or fifteen minutes, the noise died away. The last car rumbled into the distance.

Still, I wanted to make sure there weren't any stragglers.

Without turning on the porch light—or accidentally turning on the palm in the window—I opened the door to check.

It was completely dark now. The orange streetlights on Main Street were lit. There wasn't a soul on the porch or in the yard.

"They're gone," said a voice from behind me.

"Ingrid?" I turned.

She smiled from the landing, hopped on the railing, and rode it down like I used to do when I was younger. It drove my mother crazy, but Cora thought it was funny.

"I was watching from my window," she said. "They're gone now. All of them."

"Thanks." I met her at the base of the stairs, grabbed my bags, and it struck me. "Why didn't you let them inside? I mean, don't get me wrong, I'm glad you didn't. But they were out there knocking for how long?"

"About an hour," she said.

"And you didn't want to open the door?"

She shrugged.

"You did the right thing. I'm just curious."

"After what happened this afternoon," she said, "I figured you didn't want to do any readings."

"I don't... ever."

"You'll change your tune." The cat pranced out of the den, her tail held high. Aunt Cora scampered up the steps ahead of us.

"Do you hear her too?" I asked Ingrid.

"The cat?"

I nodded.

"Unfortunately."

"I heard that." Aunt Cora's tone was sour. Not that it was ever sweet.

I was pleasantly surprised to see the upstairs hallway was mostly free of clutter. At the top of the stairs, there was an old wicker cabinet with a few knickknacks, but the rest of the hall was clutter free. The junk I was expecting was gone.

"What happened up here?"

"Your cousin Josh," Cora said. "He cleared it out. They had an estate sale and donated the rest."

"You were okay with that?"

"It wouldn't matter if I wasn't. Josh can't—or won't—hear me in this form. And I left him everything in the will except this house. So, he could do with it what he wanted—even if that was to give everything Marcy ever gave me right back to her."

"Why didn't you leave the house to Josh? He's your grandson."

"Several reasons," she said. "Josh didn't want the house. He told me as much. And honestly, that boy has enough on his shoulders as it is."

"Oh, I get it. You respect his wishes but not mine."

"If that's the way you choose to see it."

"I'm not sure there's another way."

The doors were shut, including the door to the bathroom. A single sconce cast a long shadow on the wall.

Somehow, Ingrid maneuvered around the shadow. She came to a halt in the middle of the hallway, next to a painting that looked like a cross between a Van Gogh and a Picasso, in the worst way possible. It was obviously something Cora had traded for a reading. Josh hadn't found it a new home.

The first door was Aunt Cora's room. The second was where my mother and father lived when his cancer took a turn for the worse, and where my mother stayed long after.

Across the hall was the bathroom shared by all. And at the end of the hall was the smallest room—the room that used to be mine.

"That's mine now," Ingrid said as my eyes lingered on the old door. Its paint was chipped and as faded as the wallpaper.

"I guess that means I get one of these two?"

"As if it's a choice." The cat leaned against the first door. "My bed's the best in the house. And you know as well as I do, there're a lot of memories buried in the other room."

"You didn't have to say it out loud," I said.

"You're right," Ingrid agreed. "But you were already thinking it pretty hard. Your forehead's all creased up. Better stop, or it'll stick that way."

"It will not."

"The line will. If you aren't careful."

I rolled my eyes. "Thanks for the tip."

I put my things in Aunt Cora's room.

Apparently Josh hadn't wanted any of the furniture in

here. The bed, the dresser, and a nightstand were where they had always been. There was also a sturdy wooden desk, where normal people might keep a desktop computer. Aunt Cora kept a ceramic bowl there.

I knew what it was, although I'd never actually seen her use it. The scrying bowl was for divination, much like a crystal ball.

Practitioners fill the bowl with water and stare at the glassy surface, usually to see into the future but sometimes to look into the past.

It sort of creeped me out because I knew Cora passed away in here. I'd seen her, just above the scrying bowl, in a vision.

And she knew it.

"Don't dawdle over there. It's not like my ghost is going to jump out and bite you."

"That's not funny."

"What's not funny?"

"You're a cat. You could literally jump up and bite me."

"I said jump out. Not jump up. And why would I bite you when I've got these glorious claws to scratch you with?"

I glowered at her. "You're sleeping somewhere else tonight."

"I most certainly am not. This is still my house. My bed. My rules."

"Nope." I shook my head. "Legally, the house—and everything in it—belongs to me."

The cat crouched, readying for a leap onto the high bed. She wanted to prove me wrong. She sprang forward, gaining altitude, when something distracted her. She twisted sideways and crashed into the mattress, landing on her feet on the floor.

"What was that?" Ingrid and I asked in unison.

"That was something we won't speak of again," Cora said.

I stifled a laugh. "And?"

"And someone's outside," she said sourly.

"Again?"

Yet again, someone was knocking on Cora's door, and I had to decide whether I wanted to answer it.

7

I took the stairs by twos, like a kid—a kid twenty years removed. I slid on the landing and nearly tore my ACL.

That slippery hardwood had once been fun. Not anymore. I took the rest of the stairs more carefully.

The knock at the door wasn't frantic, but it was persistent. Three more knocks boomed through the foyer.

I swore under my breath.

If it was Gladys or Marcy again—or Colleen—they were going to get that door slammed in their face and an earful. Then slammed in their face again.

I flipped the porch light on, careful not to touch the *other* light—the light that had started this nonsense.

I opened the door a crack.

The woman outside wasn't Gladys, Marcy, or Colleen.

"Good evening, Willow."

A stern voice from a sterner face, deep set lines pulling dark red lipsticked lips into a permanent frown. But then she'd never liked me.

"Uh... Good evening, Mrs. King."

Of anyone I could have imagined showing up on this doorstep, she was the least expected. Then again, she was Beau and Alaina's mother.

"How can I help you?" I asked.

"You know I have no interest in a palm reading. Or tarot cards. Or whatever else Cora got up to in this place."

"Right." No surprises there. She and Aunt Cora never got along.

"I want *your* help."

Briefly, I thought about closing the door on her face and my insides squirmed. This was the moment that other psychic—Scarlett Myst or whatever—alluded to earlier.

Had I just taken her advice...left and never looked in the mirror.

Why hadn't I? Pride? Or stubbornness? Both?

There were few people in Mossy Pointe who mattered, as far as I was concerned. Nikki and Henry always, but never Alaina or Shawna.

Mrs. King... She did.

I thought about how many suppers I'd eaten at her house. After school, we used to go over there to play on Beau's Nintendo 64. She'd get home, tired from a long day's work, and send Beau and Alaina to do their chores but fuss over the rest of us.

Maybe it was time I paid all those years of kindness back.

Still, I was reluctant. I had no way of knowing what was going on—what had happened to Perry or why the police thought Beau was responsible.

"Can you help me?" Mrs. King asked.

"I—I already told Alaina I don't do that kind of thing."

"Were you listening to me, child? I'm not into that stuff. You're a cop, aren't you?"

"A deputy." *A deputy on a leave of absence and well outside my jurisdiction.*

"Tomayto, tomahto. I need your help. Beau needs your help."

"I don't have any authority here, Mrs. King. It's not my jurisdiction. Or my case."

"Then make it your case. You can investigate, can't you? Ask some questions. We need a second opinion. As far as everyone around here is concerned, it's an open and shut case."

I struggled to find an answer. She was right. I could ask a few questions. It wouldn't do any harm.

"We can pay you for your trouble."

That hit a nerve. I owed this woman. I owed her much more than money could buy.

"I'm not some private eye out to make a buck off your troubles," I said.

"No. You're better than that." Her frown deepened. "Now, can I come in?"

"Of course," I said. "I'm sorry. I forgot my manners."

"No. It's me who's sorry." She scooted past me, much like her daughter had earlier that day.

Mrs. King was on the heavier side. She wore her hair in a short, feathered bob. She was dressed in a sleek garnet suit with a black blouse. She looked like she'd come from work.

About ten miles outside of town, there was a dog toy factory. Mrs. King had worked her way up from the floor to an upper management position.

"What do you mean, you're sorry?" I asked her. "What do you have to be sorry about?"

"You didn't ask for any of this." She indicated the house. "It was thrust upon you. Now, here I am, piling on. But I wouldn't be asking you if it wasn't dire. We're desperate, Willow. Mr. Green wants Beau to take a plea deal."

"Mr. Green's representing Beau?"

She opted for the den over the parlor. I clicked on a lamp while she chose a seat, dusted it off, and sat.

I took a spot on the couch across from her.

"Of course he is," she said. "Artie Green is the only lawyer in town. The only lawyer in the area worth much of anything. Not that I've spoken to him, mind. It's always that secretary of his, Marge. Either way, they think Beau should take the deal the prosecutor's offering."

"What is it?"

"It doesn't matter what it is. Beau didn't do this. He's already spent more time in jail than he deserves."

"Okay. But I have to ask—what do they have on Beau?"

"Nothing," she said flatly.

"They have to have something."

"What did Marge say?"

She tapped her foot. "I think she said it's circumstantial. They had probable cause because of some financial affairs between the two of them—Beau and Perry. I don't know what that's about. I'm sorry. You'd have to ask Beau. Then there's his whereabouts at the time of the murder."

"And where was he?"

"Well... They don't know. That's the thing. He turned off his phone."

My own phone buzzed in my hand. I looked to see who was calling, grimaced, and sent the call to voicemail. He wasn't going to like that.

"You need to answer that?" Mrs. King asked.

"He'll call back," I said.

"Willow, I know you. I know we're talking about something serious right now. But that phone call was serious too. I saw the look on your face."

"It's nothing," I said.

"Husband?"

I nodded.

"You're right." She sighed. "He *will* call back. You left him in Virginia?"

"It didn't make sense for both of us to come down," I said like I'd rehearsed it. "I'm supposed to be tying up loose ends. We plan to sell this place. I don't even know why Cora left it to me."

"I'm going to have to say it again, aren't I?" She brightened. "I know you. I know when you're lying—just like I knew every time y'all told your mommas you were staying over at my house and went out to Lord knows where. I lied for you then. If you want to lie to me now, that's fine. But you *do* know why Cora left you this place. You just aren't going to tell me. And that's fine."

I smiled weakly. "Nothing gets past you, huh?"

"Nothing much," she said. "But this did. Whatever Beau and Perry were up to—I know my boy. I know he didn't do this."

"I understand."

"You understand more than most. You also understand the uphill battle he's facing."

"I do," I admitted. "I'm just not sure I can be much help. Like I said, I'm here tying up loose ends. I have to get back to Virginia. The sooner the better."

My phone began to buzz again. I ignored it.

She smiled thinly, shaking her head. "Keeping up an old house like this is a full-time job. I wish you luck."

"Thank you," I said. "And I wish you and Beau luck. If he really isn't guilty, I'm sure this will work out." I could practically hear the lack of sincerity in those words. She was right. He was facing an uphill battle whether he was to blame or not.

Mrs. King didn't bother to reply. She picked up her purse and stood.

Looking up at her face sent me elsewhere—to a time when Beau and I were good friends. When I cared deeply for him. When I thought I loved him.

By the time she got to the front door, I relented. "Fine," I said. "I'll do it."

She turned, a look of bemusement on her face. "You'll do what?"

"I'll look into it. For you. And for Beau."

She sighed with relief, as if my help might actually mean something.

"I'm not promising anything," I told her.

"You don't have to." Her eyes welling up made me want to squirm. "I know you, Willow Brown—what kind of person you are. If you say you'll do it, then you're gonna do it. You'll get the job done. You'll get my boy free."

I wanted to warn her that the opposite might be true. If Beau *did* do it, I'd find that out too. And I'd turn over any evidence I found.

I let those words go unsaid.

I waited for her to get in her car and start it, then I flipped the porch light off.

Instead of marching upstairs, I went outside and took a seat on the steps.

The town was shrouded in darkness. The tall pines hid the moon. A light overcast hid most of the stars. Frogs, crickets, and other nightlife filled the air with their nightly orchestra.

My phone buzzed for a third time. For a second, I considered sending him to voicemail again.

Instead, I answered.

FROM <u>*NEIGHBOR SLEUTHS*</u> *post Justice for Perry Robinson...*

StrangerThanFiction (Top User): Finally! Justice has been served.

A_M_Lee (Admin): What? Who? Where are you getting your information?

Kirk-JD: Stranger's going to make us wait...

BellaBella: Someone's been listening to their police scanner again.

Tooomz (Admin): I heard it too. They took Beau Robinson into custody. No word if it's actually related to Perry's murder.

StrangerThanFiction (Top User): It is.

Admin12355: It is.

Kirk-JD: Source? No way Beau did this.

BellaBella: I still haven't heard anything else. Pinging @GrannyMarge

Admin12355: Trust.

StrangerThanFiction (Top User): Sorry. I'm tied up at the moment. Will get you all the details when available.

Kirk-JD: Literally tied up? Do you need our assistance? :P

A_M_Lee (Admin): Please stay on topic, JD.

Kirk-JD: Fine... I still don't believe Beau could do this.

Tooomz (Admin): Me either. But we're all capable of something.

ScarlettMystic: Signs point to his innocence.

Admin12355: lol, signs point to your lunacy.

GrannyMarge: I'm here. It does look like charges are imminent. I can't post about the case. You understand.

Tooomz (Admin): We do. Thanks, Marge.

Admin12355: So he's guilty. Obviously.

BellaBella: Any proof to speak of besides your obnoxious behavior in our chats?

Kirk-JD: Proof?

Admin12355: I'm on the internet. I don't need proof. That's internet 101.

Tooomz (Admin): While you're free to speak your mind here, we will block you for trolling.

Admin12355: You can't block me. I'm an admin. What I say goes!

A_M_Lee (Admin): Just because your handle says admin doesn't make you an admin. I can and will block your posts.

Admin12355: Can you though?

A_M_Lee (Admin): Done.

BellaBella: Anyone else have something to say about Beau and his arrest?

Kirk-JD: I'm waiting to hear details.

Tooomz (Admin): Same.

Admin12356: Ha! I'm back!

A_M_Lee (Admin): Are you though?

BellaBella: I hate trolls.

A_M_Lee (Admin): Bahahahaha... I blocked his IP Address. He won't be back for a while.

StrangerThanFiction (Top User): Press conference tonight. Local news will cover it. Thanks for the patience, folks.

Admin12357: Okay. I had to go to the library to post this. But I'm here again...

Admin12357: Hello?

This conversation was archived by an admin.

8

There was a cat on my chest. It had to weigh at least twenty pounds. Its claws had penetrated my night shirt and were definitely going to leave a mark.

This was that nightmare scenario Nikki had warned me about.

On top of that, the room gave me an uneasy feeling—the universal this isn't my room, not my bed, not my house. Not really.

I tossed and turned all night long, waking up in the middle of the night to scroll through the community chats about Perry's murder.

This morning, I wanted to stay in bed and mind-numbingly scroll through social media—posts about anything other than murder cases, like recipes and funny raccoon videos. But the cat was ruining any notion of that.

After I got off the phone with Tim, Aunt Cora had given me some space, allowing me to bathe and perform my nighttime routine in some peace.

The reprieve was over.

"What are you doing?" I tried to move the cat. She didn't budge. "What is it you want?"

"She's hungry and she wants to go out. In that order."

"Who?" I asked. "You? You want to go out?"

"The cat," she hissed. "Maybe I didn't explain this well enough. We cohabitate in this body. I let her do what she needs to do. She lets me do what I need to do. Right now, she's hungry. There's canned food down in the pantry."

"Then she goes outside?"

"Am I the type of person to keep a litter box?"

I thought a moment. "I guess not."

"You guess right." The cat hopped down from the bed. "And if she brings you a present, you best be grateful. It's better she finds the rats than you do."

"That's fair," I said. "Do you get many rats around here?"

"We live at the edge of town, next to a swamp. What do you think?"

I didn't want to think.

I followed her—them—down to the kitchen. The pantry was mostly bare, just cans of cat food. I opened one with a manual can opener.

No electric. Of course.

Aunt Cora wasn't the kind of person to upgrade. If something served its purpose, it was good enough for her.

The cat yowled and stretched. I wasn't sure Aunt Cora was there anymore. If she was, she was quiet.

While the cat ate, I took out my phone and looked for an article about Beau's arrest. I found nothing, but I was sure it was coming.

According to the website, the local paper was staffed by just two people—the editor, Callum Hornby and a reporter, Ivy Hornby, who was either his wife or sister.

Or both.

I chuckled to myself—a town so small needs new residents.

"What's so funny?" Cora asked. The food dish was licked clean.

"Nothing," I replied. "Actually, this is anything *but* funny. These articles are grim. What do you remember about Perry Robinson's murder?"

"Was it while I was alive?" she asked.

"Yeah."

"When?"

"Six or seven months ago."

"I won't remember it," she said. "I had dementia for the last year or so. My psychic abilities were about all I had left in the end."

"Do you remember Perry at all?"

"Vaguely. He was a friend of yours, right? I believe he worked down at Mac's Auto."

"That's it? That's what you remember?"

"If he wasn't a client—or a friend of a client—why would I? It's not as if I had a car to get around in."

"But you did have a car."

"Not for years."

I scowled. "Then how do you know he worked at Mac's?"

"Because Mac mentioned it."

"You did a reading for Mac?" That sounded out of character.

"His wife," Cora said. "He came with her once."

"At least it gives me a place to start. I should probably talk to Beau too. That shouldn't be too hard. I know exactly where he's staying for the next little while. And we have the same lawyer."

The cat's tail twitched. "Sounds like your day is planned. Right. So, I must insist you allow us out into the back yard."

"The back yard?" I scowled. "You aren't afraid of snakes or gators?"

After about an acre of soggy grass, Cora's back yard sunk into a lowland swamp which was fed by a small creek, which was fed by a small river a few miles away.

When I was young, my mom always warned us not to go traipsing too close to the swamp. She had an irrational fear of alligators. Then, so did I, despite not having met one outside of a zoo.

"I'm more afraid of vehicles going above the speed limit and this dumb cat attempting to cross the road. We still have trouble with our impulses. I keep telling her the nine lives is a figurative, not literal thing."

I shrugged and let the cat scurry into the back yard. I just hoped Aunt Cora didn't end up as an alligator's breakfast.

My stomach growled in a strange sort of agreement and my vision went out of focus, misty white.

When I got a vision, it wasn't like seeing a movie or watching someone from above. Most of my visions were seen through someone else's eyes—like I was a passenger in their mind with no controls.

I had to put together clues to figure out whose eyes I was seeing through. It was usually pretty easy because it was the person I'd last touched.

This time, I hadn't touched anyone.

And this time, it was easy. I was more familiar with these eyes than any other pair. And with the bare feet in the grass.

My feet.

I saw myself standing in the back yard, holding up my phone. It was ringing.

I waited for the vision to play out.

Growing up, I'd always tried to suppress my visions. I

never got especially good at it, but eventually, I could snuff out two or three out of every ten.

It was much harder if the vision came on after touching someone.

There were times when I had to stop a vision—like when I was driving. Something about going rigid and blind while operating a vehicle at fifty-five miles per hour didn't sit right with me.

So, if I sensed it coming on soon enough—the white blur narrowing my vision and my joints locking up—I could fight it. I could squint my eyes, clench my fists, and force my mind to go blank.

But I don't do that anymore. Because the last time I suppressed a vision, I missed something big. The last time it happened was the day my husband got stabbed.

———

THE VISION WAS A SHORT ONE. The conversation on the phone equally so.

When the vision left me, I realized I was crying. And the phone was ringing.

I couldn't do this.

I had to do this.

I knew who was going to be on the other end of the line. I knew what he was going to say. I even knew what I would say in response.

I would say things I'd regret.

No, I won't.

The phone continued to ring with Tim's special ringtone — "All My Life" by K-Ci & JoJo.

I answered. "Hello?"

"I asked you to call me this morning."

"It's still morning." I automatically went on the defensive —just as I had in the vision. "I've been busy. You're aware the phone works in both directions, right?"

"I'm aware," he said. "Hence me calling you right now. Hence me calling you last night after what, a day of not speaking?"

Damn.

He was so frustrating. I couldn't articulate exactly why I was mad at him. Originally, I wanted him to come on this trip. But when he'd offered, I turned him down. I was the one who told him not to come.

Now, it seemed like I resented that he hadn't insisted.

"You doing okay this morning? How's the house? You get a good night's sleep?"

"Not really." I walked out into the yard, letting my toes sink in the wet grass. "The house is everything I told you about and more. I don't think there's anything here I want."

"And the roommate—she still there?"

"For now," I said.

"You gotta figure that out." He sighed into the phone. "If I was there, she'd be gone."

"But you're not here. It's just me."

Why am I letting the vision play out? I can stop it.

"And whose fault is that?" His tone wasn't unkind, which only made it worse.

"Can we not?" I squeezed my toes together and felt a *squish.*

"Fine with me," he huffed. "But you know I would've come down there. You just had to ask."

I tried to change the subject. "How are things up there? Has the town blown up without me?"

"Not yet." He laughed. "But you know it will. They need you around here. More than anyone needs me."

"You'll find something," I said.

"You keep saying that. Here I thought you were supposed to be good at predicting stuff."

Tim was yet another person who didn't know about my gift. Not really. He knew people thought I could predict things. And I'd told him a little about Aunt Cora. He knew I had episodes—something like epilepsy but not.

But Tim was a regular guy. We lived in a town full of paranormal activity, and he didn't know any of it existed.

Tim had been an officer with the Creel Creek Police Department.

In Creel Creek, the city cops deal with the normal crime. The Sheriff's Department take on the more unusual cases—cases of the supernatural variety.

Now I fear the normal crimes most.

It had been a normal day when a vision started to come on and I suppressed it.

TIM WAS APPREHENDING A NORMAL SUSPECT. He was stabbed in the leg and twice in his side. His recovery took months. But even with his leg recovered to around ninety percent, it wasn't enough. The department cashed him out on a medical and gave him a small pension.

After that, things between us changed.

He blamed himself.

I blamed myself.

It didn't make for a good situation.

Had I just let it happen—let the vision play out, I could've prevented it.

Instead, I got a phone call telling me Tim was in the hospital. He'd lost a lot of blood. He needed surgeries —multiple.

He could blame himself all he wanted, but it was my fault.

"I've been thinking a lot." There was a hint of brightness in his tone, almost like he knew I'd flipped the conversation with my subject change. Like he'd also seen it going down that dark path. And now it hadn't.

"Haven't I told you that's dangerous?" I asked, smiling into the phone.

"You've mentioned it a time or two."

"What have you been thinking about, Timothy Brown?"

"About us," he said. "About our future."

"And?"

"I'm not sure it's here. In Virginia, that is."

"It's not?"

"I wish I'd gone with you," he said. "I want to see this place. Maybe this house is just what we need—what we need to start fresh."

"Don't get too far ahead of yourself." I turned to look up at the blueish-purple siding, some of it in desperate need of repair. "This house is a wreck. It's old and it's musty. And it's some weird shade of purple or blue or both. You'd hate it."

"I know how to buy paint, Willow. What about the town? I know what you've said, but it can't be much different from Creel Creek."

"Uh... It's about as different as it comes. It's small—much smaller, if you can imagine. And it's in Florida. Home of the Florida man."

"I resent that. I was originally a Florida man."

"You lived in Miami until you were six. That doesn't count. Miami isn't really a part of Florida."

"Technically, it is."

"Technically." There was no winning an argument with Timothy Brown—not with him on his game. And today, he was on his game. "I'll give it some thought, okay? But my gut says we sell this house and use the money to pay off ours."

"Or," he offered, "we sell both. With that and my pension, we can find someplace in West Virginia and live off the grid."

This was our joke.

"You wouldn't survive two days off the grid."

"That, my dear, is the God's honest truth. Call me tonight, all right?"

"I will," I promised.

I hung up and for a moment, felt at peace with the world.

Then the cat wallowed out of some shrubs and placed an offering at my feet. My bare feet.

The rat spasmed with its dying breath, and I shrieked and ran to the house.

It touched me!

9

Ingrid was a good roommate. From what I could tell, she was quiet and kept to herself. Her side of the bathroom was clean. Spotless. If she wasn't in the room with me, it was almost like she wasn't there at all. I really hated forcing her out of the house.

I hadn't heard a peep from her all morning. The TV wasn't on in her room.

I gathered that she was the type of roommate who stored food in her bedroom rather than in the pantry downstairs. She probably had a hotplate or something.

After washing my feet and rinsing my brain of the past few minutes, my stomach reminded me in no uncertain terms of the need for sustenance. But there wasn't much there: some stale cereal, a sleeve of saltine crackers, and various cans of soup.

The fridge held a few sticks of butter, a withered pineapple on a shelf, and some rotted vegetables in the drawer. But there was a carton of eggs. They were near enough to their date to chance them.

After cracking a couple and smelling them carefully, I

put enough butter in the pan to disguise them if they were off.

Ingrid trudged into the kitchen and slumped at the kitchen table, looking groggy.

"Rough night?"

She glared up at me. "A bit."

"Everything okay?" I asked. "Something you need to tell me about?" I wondered if she had been searching for a new place to stay.

"You know you snore, right?"

The whisk in my hand clattered a little louder. "I believe my husband might've mentioned it a time or a thousand. The walls are that thin, huh?"

"Like paper," she said.

That reminded me of something but for the life of me, I couldn't jar it loose.

Then it hit me. Marge Kenner said the mailman would deliver that paperwork. And I never checked the mail. "You didn't happen to get the mail yesterday, did you? I'm expecting something."

"I don't get mail." Ingrid had a funny look on her face as if the idea of her getting mail was something odd.

"Ever?"

"Not in a while."

"So, you don't check it?"

She shook her head.

I understood where she was coming from—most of my bills were digital these days. The mail I did get was junk— offering to lower my bills, consolidate my credit card debt, or asking for donations. Mostly a giant waste of paper.

Still, it hadn't occurred to me that I'd have to go through Cora's mail. It still didn't feel like my house. I supposed it never would, especially not after I signed the papers for Mr. Green.

I went to the table, loaded a plate with eggs. They steamed as I tipped the pan in Ingrid's direction, offering her the rest.

She waved them off.

"Okay. So, you don't, uh, order things online or whatever?" I took my seat.

She shrugged. "If I did, they'd be on the porch."

"True. Everything I get in the mail is junk anyway."

"Except today. You said you're expecting something?"

I had to level with her. "Today is different," I admitted. "It's about the house. I'm going to sell it. I'm guessing you haven't found another room for rent, have you?"

She looked dubious.

"You haven't looked?"

"Honestly, no." She lifted her head from the table and met my gaze. "But that's just because I know there's nothing available. I looked everywhere before Cora opened her door to me."

That was an odd way to put it.

But nothing she was saying surprised me. It was like Mrs. Kenner had told me. There was no housing market here. With no housing, there was no rental market either.

But there had to be somewhere she could go.

If only she could buy the house and solve all my problems.

On my walk to Sabal's Grill, I'd seen what Mrs. Kenner described. Off the main road, there were a couple of houses with for sale signs, mildewed and hardly readable with ivy growing up their posts.

There was *also* mildew splattered across the mailbox of

2002 Main Street. Worse, it was too close to the road, and there were cars whose drivers had no respect for the law.

For years, this place had been a speed trap. There'd always been a police cruiser hidden near the speed limit sign. But now that I thought about it, I hadn't seen any law enforcement since getting here.

The house straddled the city limits, right where Main Street officially reverted to Highway 83. There were miles of pine trees and swamp until the turn off to the river, then several more miles before hitting the coast.

A car zoomed past, going nearly double the limit.

Yanking down the reluctant door, I found the mailbox full to the brim with packages and envelopes, including a manila envelope I assumed to be from Artemis Green's office.

I tucked as much as I could in the crook of my arm and checked the road before shoving my hand inside to get the stragglers.

The edges of my vision went white.

I froze there, with my hand deep inside the mailbox. I had one foot on the grass. The other was about a foot onto the roadway.

I hate visions.

I hated even more the thought of suppressing it and missing something important.

It took longer than usual to get my bearings—I had to figure out where I was and whose eyes I was looking through. They weren't my own this time.

This person was taller. And they needed to see an eye doctor—or I thought so because their vision was so blurred. Then I realized it was smoke causing their eyes to water.

Thick black smoke billowed from behind double doors.

I knew those doors—the double doors to the kitchen at Sabal's Grill.

These were Nikki's eyes.

Smartly, she put a palm to the door to check the heat level. Satisfied, she shouldered into the kitchen. Smoke filled the space, black and choking thick. It poured from all directions, making it hard to find the source.

She struggled a few feet and found a strip of the back wall was aflame, burning bright orange. The back door was open. Fire was licking the frame.

The rest of the kitchen was okay. The fire hadn't yet found the grease trap.

Nikki bent down, struggling for breath. She searched for Henry who was nowhere to be found. She rounded the prep tables and scoured the floors.

"He's not here," I tried yelling to her. But this was a vision. She couldn't hear me.

Henry must've gotten out through the door, which gave her—and me—some relief.

She retreated out the double doors and through the front of the building, not through the flames near the back door. A crowd had gathered in the parking lot.

Coughing, Nikki asked, "Have you seen Henry? Has anyone here seen Henry?"

There were a few shrugs and a head shake.

Nikki coughed again and spun on her heels. He was still somewhere out back.

She ran down the side of the building, past the dumpster, through the brambles and onto the dirt path. She passed her Mustang and Henry's work truck.

In the grassy alley behind the large building, home to several businesses, not just Sabal's Grill, there was an old smokehouse where Henry's father had barbecued the Wednesday specials—ribs and pulled pork.

Obviously, Henry had continued the tradition.

The smokehouse was nothing more than a shed—a screened-in shack around a giant metal smoker. Split wood was stacked around it.

All of it was on fire and likely what started the whole thing, spreading through the grass to the back of the building. Thick plumes of smoke billowed into the air. The smell was overpowering, and Nikki began to choke.

She sputtered and coughed and wiped her eyes, and when the smoke shifted slightly, she finally saw her husband.

Henry was sprawled half inside, half outside the shed. The screen door had closed on him. His head and an outstretched arm had made it out of the squat building, away from the smoke and flames. A fire extinguisher had rolled free of his hands.

For a second, Nikki was relieved. She'd found him. But it wasn't clear if he was even alive. And he was bleeding from somewhere on the side of his head.

He wasn't safe.

While the fire had yet to reach him, the roof of the shed threatened to collapse. It bowed and buckled, putting him in a precarious situation.

"Henry," Nikki called.

She reached down and put his arm over her shoulder, attempting to drag him away, but she couldn't manage his weight.

A few seconds later, someone came from behind and helped pull Henry to safety.

He was safe. *Safer.*

The vision faded away without telling me Henry's fate.

I blinked.

My hand was still inside the mailbox.

A car zipped past, wind fluttering my shirt. They laid on the horn.

"Get out of the road, idiot," the passenger yelled.

They gave me the finger for good measure.

Again, I had to get my bearings. I shielded my eyes and looked down the street toward Sabal's Grill.

There was no smoke in the air. Not yet. Which meant there was still time for me to stop the fire from happening.

10

Sabal's Grill was what my mom would call a good mile away. A good mile is hard to define—somewhere between three-quarters of a mile and a mile and a half. It had easily taken me twenty minutes to walk there the previous day.

Why I thought running there was a good decision, I'm not sure.

I booked it that direction. I got about a quarter of a mile down the road when it occurred to me I had a car. I gritted my teeth, kicked up the pace, and kept running because doubling back and getting my keys from the kitchen would take more time.

And time was running out.

I stretched it to my limit down the sidewalk, hoofed it across the road, and threw open the door to the restaurant like the place was already ablaze.

Nikki was waitressing this morning. Her eyes went wide at the sight of me huffing and puffing in the doorway, and she poured a pot of fresh coffee on Mr. Thomas's lap.

The old man nearly flipped the table, dancing away from it and patting himself in an unmentionable place.

"Whooo wheee," he bellowed, still jiving. "That'll wake you up."

"Oh my gosh, are you all right?" Nikki yanked napkins from the dispenser and handed them to him.

The old man took them and groused, "Sixty-six years old, and I learned something new today."

"What's that?" Nikki asked.

"I've been doing coffee wrong all these years. I always thought you were supposed to drink it."

"Funny," Nikki said, unamused. "I guess your coffee's on me today."

"Wrong again—because *your* coffee is on me. See here." He took his newspaper from the table and waved it like a fan.

"I'd rather not look at that." She narrowed her already narrow eyes at me. "What's going on? Where's the fire?"

Not here yet.

"Where's Henry?" I asked her.

I would never have believed her eyes could narrow any farther, yet they did. "You came in here like that to see my husband? Willow, I thought we were friends."

I was still in my pajamas. I shook my head. "Where is he? He might be in trouble."

"Oh, he's bound to be in trouble." She gesticulated with her empty coffee pot. "Through there. I think I heard him head out back."

I shouldn't have wasted that much time. I knew where he was—or where he'd be found. Talking to Nikki about it hadn't done either of us any good.

I grimaced, then headed for the double doors.

Maybe I can catch him in time—before he gets knocked out. Before the fire spreads to the kitchen.

I was almost to the door when I heard Henry's voice on the other side of it. "Coming through."

The doors—both of them—hit me square in the face.

FLAT ON MY BACK, I saw stars dancing on the drab ceiling of Sabal's Grill. My nose stung. I was dizzy and not sure what I was doing on the floor.

Henry's head appeared, eclipsing the stars. Nikki crowded in beside him.

"Let's get you up," she said.

With her hands guiding me, I sat up. Only then did blood trickle down my nose and across my lips. I tasted its metallic tang.

Nikki yanked more napkins from the closest dispenser and held them to my nose. "What on Earth's gotten into you?"

"I'm so sorry." Henry bent down and put a hand on my shoulder. "I yelled I was coming through. Honestly, I wasn't expecting you there."

"Why weren't you outside?" I asked. My words sounded muffled and stuffy—like my nose was feeling.

Henry shrugged. "I was outside for a second. I thought I heard someone in the shed back there. It was probably a raccoon or something. Wait...How'd you know I was outside?"

"I told her," Nikki said. "The real question is why she thought you might be in trouble."

"Honestly, I'm not sure anymore." I struggled to my feet. "Do you mind if I take a look outside?"

"Of course not," Henry said.

Nikki was of a different mind. "You need to sit down. I'll get you some water." I gave her a look. "Okay. I'll get you some Coke. Sit down. Take a minute to get yourself sorted."

"You know that wasn't a request, right?" Henry whispered.

"I'm aware," I said grudgingly.

I took a seat. That was apparently the cue. Most of the diners went back to their food. Everyone but Mr. Thomas, who was glaring in my direction, still waving the newspaper toward his lap. "I know you. Don't I know you?"

"Willow Brown," I said.

"Willow." He chewed on the word. "You related to Antony Brown?"

I shook my head. "Brown's my married name. I was Willow Jones."

"Willow Jones! I knew a Willow Jones."

"You still do," I said.

"She moved away ages ago," he said.

"And she's back now. For a limited time only."

He pointed at me. "Come by and see me. Get some honey or jam. It's the least you can do for ruining these pants."

"She didn't ruin 'em," Nikki argued, bringing me my Coke. "Coffee's not going to stain."

"They got a hole in 'em." He pointed to a worn-out spot on his thigh. "You can't tell me it wasn't the heat of the coffee that done that."

"That hole has been there for six months, Mr. Thomas. I think it might be time for a new pair of pants."

"It's a tiny hole." He shrugged, holding up his coffee cup for her to refill. This time he made sure his lap was a safe distance away.

I sipped my soda until the taste of blood was gone. I dabbed at my nose with a fresh napkin, satisfied when it came away clean.

"Now, can I look around outside?"

"Suit yourself," Nikki said. "I still want to know what that ruckus was all about."

"Me too," I mumbled to myself.

I couldn't think of a time when a vision had gotten something so wrong. Unless, for some reason, it was supposed to happen tomorrow or the next day or the next.

But that didn't seem right either. My visions were always of the immediate future. That was true for every vision except that one—the dream.

I followed Henry out the back door of the restaurant. It was exactly as it was in the vision. Minus the fire. There was the smokehouse in a mostly empty alley—an alley with plenty of hiding spots—behind trees and bushes or behind the dumpsters of the neighboring shops.

I walked the path, checking every nook, ending at the smokehouse. It was empty.

"What are you looking for?" Henry asked.

"I'm not sure."

"To me," he said, "it looked like you were looking for something. Or someone."

"That's pretty much it," I agreed.

"You care to tell me what this is about?"

"Where do you keep your fire extinguisher?"

"There's one here in the smokehouse." He opened the screen door and showed me. "There's another beside the stove. Do I pass inspection?"

I shook my head. "Sorry. It's been a weird morning."

"Funny. I thought that too. I could've sworn I heard something out here. I opened the back door, checked around, and didn't see anything. I was about to check in here, then I heard that commotion—what was that all about?"

"Nikki poured coffee on Mr. Thomas."

"Strange." He laughed.

I didn't.

That was it. The commotion had changed things. Henry never made it to the smokehouse. There was no fire. No knock to his head.

Was he going to be attacked in here? And if he was, why?

"Henry," I said. "Aunt Cora—I mean, I heard Perry worked over at Mac's Auto. Is that true?"

"It's true. What's got you thinking about him?"

"Beau."

"I see." He grinned. "Does that mean Thesaurus Brown's on the case? Get it? Like Encyclopedia but Thesaurus instead."

"I get it," I said. "And I think maybe it's best—for both of us—to forget you ever said it."

"I can't help it. Dad jokes come with the job."

"Dad jokes aside, I'm not on the case. Not really. I just told Mrs. King I'd ask a few questions. That's it."

"I see. Well, ask away."

"Talk to me about Beau? What's he been up to?"

"What hasn't Beau been up to?" Henry squinted at the sun.

"I'm not sure what that means," I said.

"Beau's been up to a little of everything. Ever since he got fired from the factory. That was a while back."

"Mrs. King didn't step in for him?"

"Who do you think fired him?" Henry asked.

"Oh…" That knowledge hit like a ton of bricks. I had to wonder what Beau could've done for his own mother to fire him from a well-paying job, with benefits. Pretty much the best gig around.

"Last I heard, he'd started a handyman business. But don't quote me on that. I never used him. I can't say the same about Perry though."

"What do you mean?"

"Perry worked on my truck. He worked on ol' Foxy over there. A couple times."

"Okay?" That didn't seem newsworthy. Mac's was the only shop in town.

Henry could tell I wasn't following. "He worked on the cars in *his* garage. Not Mac's."

"This was after he worked at Mac's?"

"Same time." Henry gestured at the old Mustang. "See, Mac's always rubbed me the wrong way. Back in 2008, he made the mistake of overcharging me. I haven't gone back since. I heard Perry was fixing cars on the side. All I had to do was order the parts and pay for his labor. Saved me a lot of money. None of Mac's hidden fees."

"That's interesting," I said.

"It is," Henry agreed. "Perry was competing with his own employer."

"Do you know if Mac ever caught wind of it?"

"I'm not sure," Henry said. "So, you're thinking what I am? You think Mac might've had something to do with Perry's murder?"

"No." I sighed. "I'm saying I can't rule it out until I rule it out."

11

Mac's Auto and Salvage was the perennial eyesore of Ox Tail Road, a main thoroughfare that connected Mossy Pointe to another state highway.

Behind a rundown fence, the salvage yard was home to row after row of broken down junkers. There were cars without tires or wheels, rusted and so overgrown with grass, it was hard to tell they were cars, let alone their make.

The garage was outside the fence. Built from cinderblock and tin, it was a low building with five garage doors—all of which were open and occupied. There wasn't a single spot without a vehicle. Two cars were up on lifts, the others were over pits getting oil changes.

I pulled into a space close to what looked like the office. It had the only people door on the building, and it was shut.

A weathered window unit rattled on a makeshift brace in the office window. I skirted it and went inside.

The air inside was slightly cooler and smelled of mildew and oil. There was a counter with an ancient cash register surrounded by stacks of paperwork and receipts.

No one was manning it. A short, redheaded boy in a torn NASCAR shirt came through the door opposite from the garage.

"Can I help you?" he asked with a slight drawl.

"I'm looking for Mac." This was my first stop helping Mrs. King, and by proxy Beau, and I already felt uncomfortable and out of place. A uniform would have boosted my confidence, but at least I wasn't in my pajamas anymore.

"You have an appointment?" The boy rubbed the back of his neck, leaving black streaks from the grease on his fingers. "We're booked up all week. Unless you need an oil change? Maybe we can squeeze you in if you give us thirty minutes or so."

"I don't need an oil change."

"What's wrong? Your car sounded like it was running good."

"It *is* running good." I tried not to let my frustration show. "No, I need to talk to Mac about something else."

"Mac's pretty busy," he said. "You sure I can't make an appointment for you?"

"Really, kid. I'd like to speak to Mac about something else. It's not about my car."

"Okay." He sounded reluctant. "Follow me."

The boy went into the garage, to an old Bronco getting an oil change. He crouched and bellowed into the pit, "Hey, uh, Mom, someone's here to talk to you."

Mom?

A face appeared from behind the Bronco's massive tires. "MJ, you couldn't get her to make an appointment?"

"She says she's not here about her car."

"I'm right here." I bent down beside him.

"Yeah, she's just right here," MJ echoed. "Ask her what she wants."

"Thanks, MJ. I can take it from here. Get back to that 4Runner."

"Yes, ma'am."

I had expected to find the owner, Macgregor 'Mac' McNamara under the vehicle. Not his daughter, Mackenzie.

She shook her head, smiling. "I heard you came back."

"Not permanently," I said.

"That's what you say." She wiped her hands with a rag. "Give me a half a second and I'll meet you up in the office."

I stood up, my knees cracking in protest. I was going to be paying for that run later. I could feel it.

Mackenzie was a year younger than me; her hair was still brown over her steel-blue eyes. We'd played basketball together in high school. She was good, all lean muscle and a great shooter.

She rattled off some instructions to MJ before joining me in the office. She had a hurried air, as if each minute was costing her something. She was still polite, and we exchanged a few pleasantries.

With the rag from her pocket, she cranked the A/C's fan to high. It made a constant high-pitched squeal for the remainder of our conversation, but the room did get cooler.

Again, Mackenzie began to wipe down her greasy fingers. It was clear she expected me to explain why I was here, although I had a feeling she knew.

"When did you take over?" I asked.

"Here?" She glanced around the office. "A few years ago. After Dad had his heart attack."

"Oh. I'm sorry. I didn't hear—"

"He's fine." She waved me off with the rag. "He moved down to the coast with Mom. He claims it was the best thing that ever happened to him. It taught him to relax."

"You don't seem to agree."

"It taught him to relax some. I just wish he'd let me take over the place for real. He comes by once a month to *check on things*," she made air quotes, "which is code for making sure I don't get rid of the junk in the scrapyard."

I nodded. "I always thought your brothers would take over this place."

"My brothers?" She cackled. "No way. They both enlisted the day they turned eighteen. They can't stand this place. Michael says he'll never do another oil change again—not after all the free labor he put in here."

"Free labor, huh? Is that your boy?" I bobbed my head in the direction of the garage.

"I'll have you know, MJ gets a quarter over minimum. But this isn't for him either. I'll be looking for a new assistant in a couple of years." She drummed her fingers on the counter. "Your Honda make the trip down okay? Where are you at again? New York? DC?"

"Virginia."

"Virginia is for lovers." She smiled. "That's all I know about Virginia. I saw it on a T-shirt."

"It's pretty up there." I agreed. "Prettier than here. Fewer stinging insects. Cooler nights."

"Sounds lovely." Her fingers continued to tap on the desk. "But I'm guessing if this isn't about that old Honda you're driving, it's about Perry Robinson."

"Sort of. I'm trying to get a clear—"

"Willow." The pleasant tone in her voice was gone. "There's no *sort of*. It's either about Perry or it isn't. I'm active enough on social media to know what you do for a living. You're not a psychic like your aunt. You're a cop. And I remember you and Beau. In fact, I always thought there was something there. I thought you two would—"

"I haven't even talked to Beau," I told her. "I'm asking questions for his momma. For Mrs. King."

"You're starting here, huh."

It wasn't a question, but I answered anyway. "I'm starting here. This was where Perry worked, right?"

"Forty-five hours a week. Built in time and a half. It still wasn't enough for him. He did a little work on the side. I know that. The chief came in and talked to me about it too. So did a few deputies. I opened my shop to law enforcement. They even checked the lot for the missing murder weapon. They didn't find a thing. I've been nothing but forthcoming with them. Same with you. Ask me anything. But make it quick. I do need to get back to work."

"I understand." Mackenzie was saying all the right things—making me all the more suspicious.

Funny that on my drive down Ox Tail Road I'd speculated about her father committing the murder. On my drive back, I'd have a new suspect in mind. Unless she could point the finger at someone else—which would draw my suspicions back to her. But it would also give me another rabbit hole to go down.

The thing about empty rabbit holes—there was usually a fat fox lurking in a den nearby.

I chose my words carefully. "So, you had no problems with Perry moonlighting? Isn't that stealing business?"

She raised her palm. "Look around, Willow. We've got plenty of business. We're always booked up. If anything, he was easing our burden. I didn't mind that. It was his *other* activities that drove me up a wall."

"Other activities?"

She picked up the rag and began wringing it, twisting it into knots and undoing them. "Perry liked to gamble. I imagine that's why he needed the money. He was always betting on something or heading up to the casino."

"Who was he betting with?"

She sighed, looking away. She knew the answer was going to pain me. And I knew the answer before it left her mouth. "It was Beau. From what I understand, he was running some sort of side hustle as a bookie. It's why his momma fired him from the factory." Her eyes found mine again. "And it's why everyone thinks he did it."

12

Often in an investigation, things went unsaid, either forgotten or withheld intentionally. When she came to me for help, Mrs. King had chosen the second path.

I wished Mrs. King had been the person to tell me about Beau's side hustle. It wouldn't have come as such a shock.

If she had, I wouldn't have gone this far. I could rationalize that I fulfilled my end of the bargain. I asked questions. I got answers.

They weren't the answers either of us hoped for.

And there was still the fire. The averted fire. The vision of a fire that never happened. Was it just an accident Henry would've had? Or was there something else—someone else?

None of it mattered. I was at a dead end with no more suspects and many more questions. The list of people I wanted to talk to was a short one. I could count them on one hand: Beau himself, someone at the police department, and witnesses, if there were any. I suspected there weren't.

I thought maybe Josh could help. I hadn't spoken to my cousin—second cousin—since my arrival. But if I did speak to him, I'd have to talk about Aunt Cora and the house. The whole messed up situation.

It wasn't a conversation I was ready to have. But the thought of another day of this—of one more day here—was mentally and physically draining.

I sat on Aunt Cora's front porch, not ready to go inside and cope with anything. I hated this town. I hated this house. I wanted it all to go away.

My phone lit up. It wasn't anyone I expected—not Josh, not my husband, not Nikki or even Marge at Mr. Green's office.

It wasn't a welcome caller. But I couldn't not answer. I smiled to myself. The caller didn't appreciate my use of double negatives.

She was labeled The Weather Woman in my phone for reasons, well, for reasons.

"Hi, Momma."

"Willow, honey, why does my phone tell me you're in Florida?" There was water running in the background. It sounded like she was doing dishes.

I always meant to turn off the find my family and friends feature. I always forgot. "Probably because I'm in Florida. Remember? I told you about Cora's house."

"Yes. You inherited it. I remember that conversation."

"I came down to claim it. And put it on the market. I told you my plans last week."

"Did you? I don't remember."

"I promise I did."

"I had a busy week last week." She never had a busy week. She was retired. Her idea of busy was binge watching a new show.

"Either way, that's what I'm doing. That's why I'm here in Florida."

"Well, good luck selling that place. My cousin Ginny says there isn't even a realtor in town anymore."

"You talk to Ginny?"

"I see her posts on social media. It's the same thing."

"It's not," I said. "And she's right. There's no realtor."

"Uh huh." She wasn't paying attention anymore. The noise on the other end of the line got louder. "How does Timothy like Mossy Pointe?"

"Tim didn't come with me." I winced, hoping maybe she was too distracted to hear it.

No such luck. The water stopped. "You left your husband in Virginia?"

"He didn't want to come."

"No?"

"We're dealing with some stuff right now. We've been dealing with stuff. You know this."

"It sounds to me like you *aren't* dealing with it."

"You know what I mean. Things haven't felt right since —well, you know. He's having trouble since the retirement. We both are."

"It's a marriage, honey. Of course you're going through some stuff. You always will be. It's one thing after another."

"Okay, Miss Marriage Guru. Tim and I have been together twice as long as you and Dad were."

"That's true. But we had kids."

"What's that supposed to mean?"

"It means we operated on kid time—it's like dog years. Seven years for every one."

"I'm not sure that math checks out."

"Don't you go correcting your momma. Now, I want to hear all about the house and the happenings down there. Don't leave out a single detail."

I left out many details—the talking cat and Perry's

murder among them. For a while, it seemed like she was paying attention, but inevitably, her mind began to wander.

"Momma," I said, hoping to get her attention again. "Do you remember Beau King?"

"Of course I do. There was a time I thought—"

"Momma," I cut her off. "Do you think he'd be capable of murdering someone?"

"I think I heard about this. Was it Perry? Did he do it?"

"I—I don't know. That's what they're saying."

"Is that what you say?"

"I don't know him anymore, Momma."

"Fair enough. Don't you get wrapped in it. Take care of your business and get out of there. This is just Mossy Pointe trying to drag you in."

"I won't get wrapped up," I lied.

"I can hear the lie in your voice," she said. "But I trust you to do the right things. You always have."

I smiled. "How's everything with you? How's Seattle?"

"Oh, you know. Same ol' thing. I need a new jacket. It's so chilly here. No matter the season."

"It's hot here all the time. And not a good heat either. It's like breathing soup."

"That reminds me, make sure you take your umbrella if you go out tomorrow. Looks like you're going to get some rain. Not as much as us, mind you. But a few showers." There it was. She couldn't go a whole conversation without checking her weather app and comparing her forecast with mine.

"Thanks for the tip."

The faucet turned on again. "I've got to finish these dishes. Talk soon. All right?"

"All right. Bye, Momma."

She hung up, leaving me to ponder what to do with the rest of my day.

There were things to do for the house—papers to sign. But there was also Aunt Cora inside. I was safer here on the front porch, unless Ingrid decided to let the cat out.

I was hungry. I could go back to Sabal's and try to explain my behavior this morning. I could try to get more answers and fulfill my promise to Mrs. King.

I couldn't let this thing run on for days. Momma was right—this mess was Mossy Pointe trying to dig its nails into me. I had to get the answers and get out.

It was time I talked to someone in law enforcement and found out what evidence they had against Beau.

13

Mossy Pointe town hall was smack dab at the center of Main Street. It was a small white building. It was squat and square and looked almost like a government building—but more like its architect had overheard what a government building should be, then winged it.

Right next door was the volunteer fire station—the only intersection in town with a light—a blinking yellow. The city buildings were across the street from the school, home of the Mossy Pointe Gators, a K-12.

I went through the doors into a foyer with a directory and a couple of display cases holding a few trophies. Framed clippings decorated the walls, all from the local paper. All but one were government related. The odd clipping featured the girls' basketball team the year we were runners up at state. I found myself in the team photo.

A hallway opened off the foyer and I started exploring. The first door opened on a conference room. There was a projector on a cart parked by the door. I inspected the paper stacked next to it. An agenda from five years ago.

I popped my head in and out of the next few rooms, finding a closet and a couple of other storage rooms. I realized I should've looked at the directory.

Next was a set of restrooms, then finally, an office. There was a desk for a secretary in front of a pair of offices.

The door to the left had Mayor James "Jimbo" Irwin stenciled on it. It was dark. The door to the right was open just a crack, and I could hear the faint clicking of a computer mouse and someone humming. The song was unmistakably "Never Gonna Give You Up" by Rick Astley. The name on the door was Kenneth Hammonds.

The name didn't ring any bells. Unlike the mayor's— Jimbo Irwin was mayor when I was a kid. He'd looked ancient then. I couldn't even imagine what twenty years had done to him.

He was probably out of the office because he was playing bingo at the Manor—the senior living home next to the Baptist church.

I knocked lightly on Chief Hammonds's door.

"One second." The mouse clicking became frantic. It stopped. "There we go. Come in." He looked up expectantly and found someone unexpected. "Oh, hello."

He stood up, smiling, and crossed the space between his desk and the door in two strides.

He looked no older than thirty with sandy blond hair and a hawklike nose. He was tall, well over six feet and his uniform fit like it had been boiled on—large gaps between the buttons on his uniform shirt that exposed a wrinkled undershirt, both tucked into extremely tight pants that were also too short. Above the ankles too short.

"Hi," I said, a little uneasy. I don't know what I was expecting, but this wasn't it.

His desk was in disarray, cluttered with papers and other

trash. There were a dozen yellow legal pads, open and filled with scrawling as legible as his uniform was tidy.

"You know there's no secretary out there?" I pointed.

"What day is it?"

"Thursday."

He checked his watch and said, "Thursday. 2:00 pm. Mrs. Clifton has to pick up her grandson from school. I believe it's baseball practice after that."

"On Thursdays," I repeated, not knowing exactly why.

"Oh, no. She has Tuesday, Wednesday, and Thursday afternoons off. But everyone here is part-time. Everyone except me."

"And the mayor?"

"Well, he would be part-time too. If we had a mayor."

"What happened to the mayor?"

He clicked his tongue. "Heart attack. Two years ago. It happened here in this office. I don't like to talk about it much."

So, not at bingo.

"Y'all have gone without a mayor for two years?"

He shrugged. "No one wants to run. It doesn't pay anything. And I handle most everything the town needs. I'm like the backup everything around here. Last week, I was driving the garbage truck. Tomorrow, I've got to check water meters while Fred George recovers from his cataract surgery."

"You sound like a busy man."

"Some days." He reconsidered. "Most days. You caught me at a good time, though. I was just sitting down for my coffee break."

"I'm sorry. I didn't mean to intrude."

"No worries. I'll solve this solitaire tomorrow." From our side of the desk, he moved his computer monitor to show me the game he'd been playing. "Please, have a seat." He shook my hand, then gestured to the chair opposite his. "I was about to make another cup of coffee. Would you like one?"

"Oh, no. I'm fine. Thanks."

"No worries." He sat back down, swiveled in his chair, and took a Styrofoam cup from a long sleeve. He opened a cabinet to reveal a mountain of Keurig cups. He selected something and proceeded to make coffee.

Coffee in hand, he spun to face me. "First things first, is this a town or a police matter?"

"Police, I guess."

"Oh, no." His face fell from bright and cheerful to tragic. "What's happened? A burglary? A theft? Is something stolen?"

"Aren't those the same things?"

"Well, yeah. I guess so. But honestly, that's about all that ever happens here. And they don't happen too often. Can I get your name?"

"Willow," I said. "Willow Brown."

"Willow," he repeated. "Willow," he repeated again. "I'm trying to save it to memory. If only ours were wired like these." He slapped his computer monitor.

"Is it Ken or Kenny?"

He reclined his seat. "Most people call me Chief. But I suspect that's because they forget my name."

I stifled a laugh.

"I'm serious," he protested. "I have one of those faces. And one of those names. It's like the whole town forgets I exist until they need something. My wife included."

I was able to stop myself from laughing at that.

"Okay. That part was a joke," he said. "My wife's the best. She's the best cook I know. The best at Scrabble too. That's silly, isn't it? I just explained what we do on Friday nights. Which reminds me—she insists I invite anyone new to town over for dinner."

"She does?"

"It's a rule of hers. If I meet someone new, they must come over for a visit."

I arched an eyebrow. "Is that a joke too?"

"Afraid not. I don't make the rules. I just enforce them. That's a cop joke. But seriously, she loves meeting new people. And in this town, we don't meet many new people."

"No. I wouldn't expect you do. How many of these get togethers have you had so far?"

"Since moving here three years ago—" he racked his brain "—this would make three."

"A newcomer a year?"

"Well, that's the average." He shrugged. "We didn't have anyone move here that first year. I guess we were it that year. More people move out of town than in."

"I bet," I said.

As if just now realizing his desk was a mess, he scooted a few empty coffee cups into the trash bin and picked up one of the legal pads. "Now, you said you're here on police business. What can I do for you?"

"I wanted to inquire about the Perry Robinson case."

He nearly spit out his coffee. "That case? Yes. Well, I can't really speak to an ongoing investigation."

"I get it. I do. I'm actually a law enforcement officer myself."

"Wait." He held his finger to his temple. "*That* Willow. Of course. That makes sense. I was wondering if I'd run into you. As I'm sure you know, the whole town has been talking about you behind your back."

"If it's behind my back, why do you think I'd know about it?"

"Because of your gifts. Obviously. Not that I go in for that kind of thing. I'm ashamed to say I never visited your aunt's parlor. But if I'm honest, I always wanted to. I watch a lot of movies and TV. That kind of thing is always intriguing, isn't it?"

"It's not what you think it is." Not that I had a good understanding of what he thought it was—just that he was the type of person to go off what he saw from Hollywood. "It's a lot like police work actually. Not exactly what you see on TV, is it?"

"It's not," he said. "But I'm glad it isn't. My wife wouldn't let me do this job if it were actually dangerous."

I was surprised. "What do you mean it's not dangerous? Aren't you investigating a murder?"

He nodded. "Sorry. That came out all wrong. It's my first murder investigation. And hopefully my last. What I meant was, the county handles the dangerous stuff—the drugs and the smuggling that goes down on the river." He shrugged. "We don't have a police boat. Or a budget. It's just me and Mrs. Clifton here, and the janitor. And neither of them will wear a gun."

"If I understand you correctly, then why, may I ask, are you heading up this investigation?"

"Because it happened in town," he said. "Which as you know isn't that big a town. I actually heard the gunshot. I was first on the scene."

"What did you see?"

"Unfortunately, not much of anything. Perry was on his front porch—like he'd just opened the door to someone and came outside to talk."

"No one else was outside?" I asked.

"A few of his neighbors came out afterward. They hadn't seen or heard anything. Not until the shot."

I would need to check with them. Maybe they would tell me another version of the story—something they wouldn't want to tell the chief of police.

"What about cars? Did someone speed off when you got there? Anything like that?"

"I'm going to level with you because you're in law enforcement. I shouldn't be telling you any of this. But honestly, I'm not that observant. I wish I was. I didn't see a thing. I did make a note of the vehicles in the vicinity and their license plates. I can make you a copy of that."

"That'd be great." It was better than nothing.

"It won't do you much good," he said. "It's the same few cars in that part of town. They're always parked there. Then again, I guess there were others—parked there at the salon and getting lunch."

I leaned forward. "Where was this?"

"Oh. He lived just behind Sabal's Grill, across Ox Tail Road from the salon. There's a row of townhouses. I was eating lunch at Sabal's when it happened. You know Sabal's Grill?"

"I know Sabal's Grill."

"Perry's townhouse is less than a hundred yards down the road."

"Ox Tail Road?"

He nodded.

"And Mac's Auto is down at the end of it." This made things much more interesting.

"Right. That's where he worked. You've done your homework."

"You're aware he was using his garage to do some auto work on the side?"

"I'm aware." The chief steepled his fingers, twiddling his thumbs. "And I see where you're going with this. But Mac was at her garage at the time of the shooting."

"And Beau?" I asked. "Where was he?"

Chief Hammonds averted his gaze. He stared down at his computer keyboard. "I shouldn't be telling you this, but it's nothing his lawyer doesn't already know. Beau King turned off his phone about an hour before the shooting. He was somewhere near the salon. He was at the salon to fix a broken sink, I think. Both Shawna and Alaina remember him being there."

"And he left before the shooting?"

"He did. They couldn't give me a clear timeline. But his phone was off. He turned it back on a few hours later. It pinged at the south end of the county, near the turnoff for the river."

"And you don't know why he was there?"

"He won't say."

"So, he doesn't have an alibi."

"That's right. Do you know about his other activities?"

"Being a bookie?" I asked.

The chief nodded. "It gets worse. According to his own bookkeeping, Beau owed Perry a lot of money. And I mean a lot of money."

14

If anyone had heard anything in the moments before Perry's murder, it was going to be his neighbors. They hadn't been forthcoming with Chief Hammonds, but that didn't surprise me.

I knew firsthand how people acted around law enforcement. It was a self-preservation thing more than anything else—there's a reason Miranda Warning says anything you say can and will be used against you.

It's easier not to say anything at all. And with a crime of this magnitude, it's much easier to tell yourself someone else will speak up.

When you do finally get someone to fess up—to tell you they heard something outside their apartment or saw something strange—it isn't always reliable. As time passes, memories fade. They get hazy. A female voice can turn into a male voice or vice versa. A simple conversation can turn into a fight. Whispers become shouts or nothing at all.

Perry had lived in a row of townhouses across from the salon, about a quarter of a mile down the street from Sabal's

Grill, where Chief Hammonds had been eating at the time the shooting occurred.

The hairs on my neck stood on end. It occurred to me that maybe Henry had seen or heard something and not put it together.

Mac's Auto was maybe a mile away. But chances were, Mac had passed this house any number of times. She would've noticed all the different cars in the garage.

I wondered, had she been honest with me? Was she really okay with Perry's side hustle?

Beau's side gig was what landed him behind bars.

Neither of Perry's next door neighbors were home.

I rang the doorbell on the next townhome and was immediately bombarded by yaps and barks. On the other side of the door, what had to be six or seven dogs joined in a chorus of aggravation at my audacity—how dare I do something so bold as ring their doorbell?

A shrill voice rose over the yapping. "Get down. Get down. And go to your room. I'm serious. To your room. This minute."

The door swung open. A woman with frizzy brown hair acknowledged me with a put out smile. She wore a comical amount of jewelry—bead necklaces, lots of rings, and earrings the size of saucers.

A growl burst from the living room behind her. A straggler, some sort of terrier mix, trotted around a corner. The little mutt turned his head and growled before disappearing.

"That's no treats tonight, Bruggle." The woman rolled her eyes and opened the door wider. "Terriers are the hardest to train. I should know—I was a Yorkshire Terrier in a previous life."

Did she really just say that?

"Sorry, I didn't prep for your arrival," she went on. "Sometimes my visions are clouded by my afternoon nap. Another of my former traits shining through." She grinned.

"Who are you?" I was finally able to say.

"Scarlett Myst. But I think you knew that. And I, of course, know who you are, Willow Brown. I sensed your impending arrival to Mossy Pointe about a month before you came."

"You mean when the local paper ran Aunt Cora's obituary? The one stating I was her only living heir?" I had found that story when perusing the articles about Perry. "Or did you happen to talk to Marge Kenner?"

Her smile never faltered. "The universe speaks its truths in a variety of ways. But then, you know that. I know a fellow seer when I see one. Get it?" She winked. "Come in. Let's have a chat."

I couldn't be sure this was the same woman doling out threats to me the day before. She was friendly. Or as Cora used to say, she was with good spirits.

Scarlett led me to her living room, which could've passed for a regular living room if it weren't for the candles everywhere and the sickly-sweet incense burning.

Scarlett took a seat on an enormous leather recliner, leaned it back, and gestured for me to sit on the couch across from her. "I sense you have some questions for me."

"You sense it, huh?" Like it wasn't written across my face.

"The universe again. It's written on your face. Please, take a seat. The couch doesn't bite. And neither do those fellows."

What I had failed to sense, but somehow she had, were a couple of heads peeking into the living room.

"Bruggle. Pinky. Back to your room." She returned her

attention to me. "I'm a better psychic than I am a trainer. I'm sorry."

"You seem like a pretty good trainer to me. I've never seen dogs obey commands like 'go to your room.'"

"They're simple enough. They understand more than people think. Cats too. But I'm deathly allergic."

"I'm not a big fan of either. But I inherited a cat."

"Yes. That's why I honked the other day. I knew Cora had a cat. So, I couldn't come inside and talk to you. I'm so glad you found your way here though."

"Honestly, it was by accident. I wanted to ask Perry's neighbors a few questions. I guess that means you."

She nodded. "Ask away."

"Were you home when the shooting happened?"

"Unfortunately," she said. "The dogs went mad. I had a time settling them down."

"So, you didn't go outside?"

"Not at first, no. By the time I got out there, the chief of police was there. He had called an ambulance. By then, a whole crowd had gathered—some folks who were down the street eating, the girls from the salon, and I guess that's about it."

"What about these neighbors here?"

"Oh, no. I think they were at work. That's why they aren't home right now."

"I see. What about before the gunshot? You hear anything then?"

"I don't believe so," she said. "I was between clients. I might've flicked on the television for a bit."

"Could you tell me which clients you spoke to? Maybe they saw something when they were leaving." It was a stretch, I knew.

She narrowed her eyes. "Is that what this about? You

want my client list. You're opening Madam Cora's again, aren't you? Here, I thought we could be friends. I heard you turned everyone away. It was a ruse, wasn't it? Trying to throw me off my game. I won't fall for it."

"It's none of those things," I said.

She rocked out of her recliner. "I warned you things were going to go bad. I warned you to get out of town. But you're going to stay. I feel it. That's fine. That's fine. A little healthy competition is a good thing."

"Scarlett, I'm sorry. I didn't mean to—"

"It's not about what you meant. It's about the things we do. Now, I'll ask you politely to leave. Last chance."

"Or?"

Barks erupted from the hallway and several tiny figures appeared in the living room.

"Oh. That." I stood up slowly, not making any sudden movements, acting as if they were a herd of miniature T-Rex. "Again. I'm sorry. I didn't mean to offend you." To the dogs, I said, "I didn't mean to offend anyone. I'm leaving."

Frustrated, I left.

THAT NIGHT, I was able to steer clear of Aunt Cora. I went through my nighttime routine, then I remembered the promise I'd made earlier that day—to call Tim. It felt like a lifetime ago.

I was tired as all get out, but I called him anyway.

It was time I came clean, at least about some things. I had to tell him what I was up to. I wanted to relay my uneventful, and yet, oh so eventful, day to him.

With his hello, I felt a pang; I wanted to leave this place. But I knew what I would find upon my return. A home with the same problems, a marriage on the rocks, and uncomfortable friendships with people who never truly understood much about me—or ever tried to get to know me more.

That was partially my fault. I never invited anyone over for dinner—much unlike the chief who'd insisted that we iron out those plans before I left his office.

In Creel Creek, I never inserted myself into anyone's plans. I went about my daily business. I went home to my husband. That was that.

Like my mother, my boss had always called my visions a gift. He saw them as something we could use when things were dire. And while he had never asked me to try and hone them, he relied on them in certain circumstances. Sometimes, it felt as if he waited on my visions for cues to jump into action.

It wasn't a good way to practice law enforcement. I never told him as much. But I probably should have.

I explained what I could to Tim—about Mrs. King's visit and the reason I'd agreed to help.

Tim missed the point. "Beau? I know that name. That's that boy you kissed, right?"

"Not a boy. He's a man now. I don't even know what he looks like anymore. He's not active on social media."

"Oh, you know what that means. He can't be trusted."

"You're not active on social media."

"I know! That's why I said it."

"You're hilarious, I know. But this isn't a funny situation."

"Sorry. You're right. I was distracted."

"By?"

"I'm attempting to cook."

My connection with Tim was strong. I could almost turn on visions of him at will.

I reached out with what Cora might call my inner eye—or whatever part of me that held this ability.

At this distance, I didn't get much of anything. Brief glimpses, a second or two ahead.

Tim had fried a burger. It looked under-seasoned and burned to an absolute crisp. He was headed for the fridge.

"The ketchup's on the inside of the door," I said.

"Hardy har." I could tell from the sound that he had retrieved the ketchup and probably some mustard and mayonnaise too. "You know I eat late when you aren't here. It's like I forget to take care of myself—I forget to function. Why do you think that is?"

"I wish I knew."

"You don't have that trouble, do you?"

"Oh, no. My stomach wouldn't allow that. And I got a run in today." I wasn't going to tell him how or why.

"Look at you. Not that I'm surprised. You never do need me."

"Tim, that's not true." I tried to sound both reassuring and playful—and not as tired as my eyelids felt. I wasn't in the mood for an argument, especially one about how much I did or didn't need him.

The truth was, I didn't know if I needed him or not.

I wanted to need him. I wanted to feel that tug on my heartstrings again.

"You're sleepy," he said.

"It's that obvious, huh?"

"It is. I love your voice when you're tired. It's your—your sexy voice."

"Is that right?" I couldn't help but smile.

"It reminds me of when we were courting—"

"When we were what?"

"Courting."

"You mean dating?"

"No. I mean courting."

"Remind me of the difference."

"Dating is dating—it's going out and having fun. There's just one end to courting. That's marriage. I knew from the moment we met that's what I wanted. I wanted to put a ring on your finger. And I wanted the whole world to know you were mine."

"Is that true?"

"I bought a ring the week we met."

"No," I said. "You got me the ring I wanted."

"Well… I might've had to trade the other in—after I showed you something like it and you told me, I quote, 'Rings like that are gaudy and impractical.'"

"Tim! You've never told me this."

"It never came up. I was embarrassed. I might've lost a little money in the trade."

"I bet." I smiled again, despite myself. "Okay. How does this remind you of when we were quote *courting* end quote?"

"Remember when I'd spend the evenings with you—at your much nicer place—your apartment? This was back when I lived with those guys in that house. You'd kick me out at some ungodly hour, and I'd call you from the car on my way home."

"I remember," I said. "You asked me to keep you company on your drive. So you wouldn't fall asleep."

This was in Richmond. We were both just out of the academy.

"I have a confession to make," Tim said.

"Yeah?"

"It took me less than ten minutes to get home most nights. I'd sit in my driveway and pretend there was traffic on 64."

"It would've been much more believable if you took 95."

"Wait. You knew?"

"Of course I knew. I wanted to be on the phone with you just as much. Maybe more."

"Definitely not more."

I had another vision of him—this one of him letting his hamburger get cold. He leaned on our kitchen counter. I could feel him smiling.

I wanted to be there. I wanted to see his smile in person.

Part of me wanted to slip back in time—see the Tim of years ago. I knew what he was up to then, driving home on the empty freeway to sit in the driveway of that crappy house he shared with three other junior officers.

Everything seemed so much easier then.

15

"That how it's going to be then? I give you a house. I offer to teach you. And you treat me like...like I'm a pet who doesn't matter."

"What are you talking about?" I rubbed sleep out of my eyes, squinting.

The cat was almost all I could see. It had a halo of yellow light around it.

"You disappeared yesterday," Aunt Cora snapped.

"I, uh, I guess I did."

It was hot underneath the covers. Too hot, but I couldn't throw them off. By some miracle, the cat was perched on top of the comforter and not on my chest.

"If you must know," I said, "I was trying to help Mrs. King."

The cat snarled.

"I meant I'm trying to help Beau." I shook my head. "I don't get it. What's your problem with Mrs. King? And what's hers with you?"

"She thinks I'm dead."

"Technically, you are, aren't you? And that still doesn't

answer the question. She had a problem with you long before you were dead. I remember."

"I'd rather not get into it. It's a long and boring story." The cat was motionless, weighing down the comforter. "You had a vision yesterday morning."

"False alarm," I said.

"There's no such thing."

Cora understood my visions weren't entirely in my control. What she failed to comprehend was why I'd never cared to learn how to use them.

She'd surprised me the other day—telling me my father had wanted her to teach me. She knew how to trigger a response all right.

But given a day to think it over, I'd come to my own conclusion—she was lying.

"You still haven't answered my question," Cora said. "Are you planning to duck out of the house again today? Do I need to make an appointment to speak to you?"

Rather than answer her, I posed another question. "What time is it?"

She did her best shrug—but cats can't shrug. She rolled her shoulders, straightening her back. The shift was enough for me to get loose and roll out of bed.

"Attempting an escape, I see. That answers my question."

"I just wanted out of bed." I checked my phone. It was already noon. "Oh my gosh. Do you need me to feed you?"

"Ingrid did all that. We decided to let you sleep in."

"We?" I arched an eyebrow.

"Me and the cat. Ingrid doesn't care what time you wake up."

"Good. I don't care what time she wakes up either. She still needs to find a new place though."

"Yes. I saw the paperwork on the table. We thought about leaving a present on it."

"Gross."

"Ingrid thought so too."

I picked out clothes for the day. All the while, the cat's yellow eyes were on me.

"What do you want?"

"To teach you. I already told you. It's why I'm here. It's why this house is yours."

"And I'm supposed to believe my father wanted this for me?"

"You can believe whatever you want, child. It's the truth. I'd never lie to you about your father."

"Do you know why I hate them? Why I hate these—these gifts?"

"I believe I do." Her voice was a whisper. "I understand why you—"

"You might understand it, but have you lived it?"

Her yellow eyes softened.

"I was too young," I said. "Too young to understand what it meant. My second vision—let's not even talk about the first. My second vision ever and it's my father learning he has cancer.

"There was no stopping it. And I blurted it out to him like it was a good thing. Like it meant he was going to get fixed."

"Willow, I—"

"No. No. Don't try to console me. I'm well past that. What hurts the most is I do remember a gleam in his eyes when it happened. Maybe I'm making it up. Maybe it was a trick of the light. But I remember this. He was proud. But that vision was the beginning of the end."

"You can't blame them," Cora said. "Life is going to

happen whether you have visions or not. Life—it just doesn't care. What was your vision about yesterday?"

I wiped a tear from my cheek. "A fire."

"You stopped it. I know you did."

"I didn't stop it," I said. "Luck stopped it."

"Sometimes, it's the same thing."

"That doesn't even make sense," I protested, wiping my cheek again with a forearm.

"What else did you find out? Is Beau guilty? Is he innocent?"

I shrugged. "It was all dead ends. Yesterday was a waste."

"Maybe. Maybe not."

"No. I'm sure it was a waste."

"Maybe you saw or heard something that your mind didn't put together but your soul can."

"Okay. I'm really not following."

"Go get a pitcher of water. I have an idea."

"I'm not sure I like your ideas. What's this about?"

"Get the water," she said again. "I understand you don't want to learn about visions. This is something else. Something else entirely. It might help this little investigation of yours."

Reluctantly, I obeyed her instructions and returned upstairs with a pitcher of water. The cat was atop Cora's old desk, next to the bowl. "This, my dear girl, is a scrying bowl."

"I know what it is. I lived here, remember?"

"I remember you running away when I tried to teach you something. Just like you did yesterday."

"Yeah, well, my legs aren't what they used to be." And thanks to yesterday, they were sore from my run to Sabal's Grill.

"Willow." Her tone was stern. "It's time you embrace who you are. These psychic abilities—"

"I know. They're a gift."

"That is *not* what I was going to say." The cat bristled. "These abilities are a responsibility. They're our family's legacy."

"I get it." I sighed. "With great power comes..."

The cat inclined its head, not finishing my sentence.

"Uncle Ben? Spider-Man?"

"Oh. I never read those comics. I was a DC fangirl. Batman's only superpower was discipline."

"What about being incredibly rich?" I shook my head. "Forget it. What do you mean it's our family legacy?"

"These powers appear in the first born of each generation. You're meant to honor them. Guide those around you into doing the right things—into making the world a better place."

"You mean the first born woman of every generation?" In my father's generation, there'd been no women. He had no sisters and no female cousins.

"That is not what I said, is it?" The cat bent its head at an odd angle, studying my reaction.

"But that would mean..."

"He knew before you did about the cancer. Your father did his best with the time he had."

"Why didn't he ever say anything?"

"That, I don't know. But you would honor him by accepting that you have these abilities. They're your responsibility."

"You've said that. But how did you honor them? You used your gift for profit. I saw how you used it. I don't want to be like that."

"That's how you saw it, huh? Old Aunt Cora, tricking

folks out of their spending money. Never offering any *real* advice."

"I...I didn't mean it like that."

I'd struck a nerve, but the truth wasn't that simple.

I paused to reflect on those years in her house.

When I was a kid—even as a teenager with visions of my own—I'd believed Aunt Cora's readings to be lies, based in spiritual mumbo jumbo.

She knew her customers so well, she hardly had to consult the cards... or this scrying bowl.

But the more I thought about it, the more I realized that every word that came out of Aunt Cora's mouth came with truth.

It made sense. Seeing a possible future and conveying that knowledge, that was the true challenge. Outside of the paranormal community, if I were to try and tell someone what their future held, they'd never believe me. When Cora had seen a client's future, she guided them with card readings and palmistry.

People were more apt to believe in the mystical ramblings of someone like—like Scarlett Myst—than to believe the straight facts coming out of my mouth.

"I want to help people," I said. "I want to help Beau."

"You will," Cora said. "And you can do it your own way. You don't have to be like me. Not if you don't want to. Now, pour the water in the bowl, and I can show you."

I did as I was told. I poured and as I did, the cat recoiled.

"She doesn't like water," Cora said, straightening. "What do you remember about the scrying bowl?"

"I remember you staring into it."

"Is that right? And what did I see in the reflection?"

"I honestly don't know. The future, I guess."

"Wrong. Try again."

"Okay... You saw yourself."

"Warmer. But still wrong."

"Are you going to tell me in what way I'm wrong?"

"I'm not," she said. "I'm going to have you try it yourself. See what happens if you stare into that bowl for too long."

If I were to guess, it was going to be a few minutes of inspecting Mossy Pointe water quality. After that, if I got especially bored, I'd study my own reflection—all my wrinkles and blemishes.

"Take the position," Cora instructed.

I leaned forward with my hands cupped under my chin. My elbows dug uncomfortably into the hard table.

"Relax. Relax until the weight of your head is in your arms and not your neck."

There were a few specks of dirt or dust atop the water. I watched them float there a minute or so, spinning like tops.

My reflection was a shadow that slowly came into view —brown eyes, the faint glow on the brown skin of my nose, my full lips.

"Look inside yourself," Cora said. "Into your eyes. Into your soul."

"I don't even know what that means."

"It means to shut up and look inside yourself."

After a quick eyeroll, I stared into them, watching as my pupils dilated and blended into the iris, watching each eye turn completely black and void. The void was mesmerizing. The rest of my reflection blurred away into nothingness.

It felt like I was standing inside that void. Outside of myself.

I tried to shake the feeling only to realize I *was* outside of myself. When I moved, my body hadn't moved with me. It stayed in that chair, elbows on the table, head in my hands.

"What in the—"

"It's a little unnerving, isn't it?"

"It's something," I said, reaching down and touching my own shoulder. "What the heck is happening? That's my body right there, isn't it?"

"It is."

"But it's my body right here too. Right?"

I could touch myself. I held a finger to my shoulder. Weirdly, I could feel it in my finger but not in my shoulder.

"That's—that's bizarre. What is this, Aunt Cora?"

"Your spirit's no longer connected to your body. You're free to roam elsewhere."

"If I'm a spirit, then why do I feel so solid?"

"That's complicated. For now, I'll tell you this house is special. Spirits appear mortal within its proximity. If you were to go through that wall there, you'd be a specter—a spectator of life without the ability to interact with it." She indicated the wall behind me.

"If I'm solid, I can't go through that wall."

"You aren't hearing me," she said. "You're still a spirit. The house doesn't change that. If you want to go through that wall, all you have to do is think it. But don't think it right—"

I thought it.

"Now," I heard her say.

The whole of me squeezed through the wall like it had been sucked into a hose. I popped out on the other side with a clear view of the purple siding. I was on the second story, floating in midair.

There was a gentle breeze swishing through the leaves of the magnolia tree in the back yard.

Cora was right. The breeze had no effect on me.

But I wanted it to. I wanted my spirit to fly. To be as free as a bird on the wind. And suddenly, I was carried off.

A strong gust sent me tumbling into the front yard. My nonexistent feet scraped the ground. A second gust hurtled me into the road.

Maybe I didn't want to be a free spirit after all. I stopped in the middle of the road long enough to get my bearings. There was a car zooming past, a red Dodge Challenger. Its bumper was a different shade of red than the rest of it.

I waved for it to stop, forgetting that I was a ball of pure thought and energy and that the occupants couldn't see me.

It was Shawna and Alaina.

For a brief second, I was inside the car with them. Then it went on down the highway, leaving me there.

I looked down, expecting to see my body as I had inside. I was anything but solid, a shadow of myself.

I struggled to remember why I was here. And how I got here. And why.

There was a house, a purple house. It looked familiar. I didn't know why.

A cat was stalking through the yard. It stopped at the edge of the road and sat on its haunches. "Your name is Willow Brown. You're scrying right now, at a desk in the house behind me. Go upstairs. Find your body. Become one again."

"My name is what?"

"Willow," the cat said again. "You used to live in this house. Do you remember?"

I wanted to shake my head no. Then I saw a little girl run through the yard. She was being chased by a little boy. He tagged her, sending her tumbling to the ground.

"You're it," he said.

She started to cry.

The boy peered down, a look of confusion on his delicate features. He bent down low. "Willow... I... I didn't mean to hurt you. I'm—I'm sorry."

The little girl smiled mischievously. She propelled herself up, thrusting a hand out. "You're it."

She ran off. The boy laughed and ran after her. They both dissolved into nothing.

The cat was still sitting there beside the road. "Did you hear me, Willow? Go back in the house. Go upstairs. Find your body. Become one."

"I heard you," I told the cat.

But I'd heard something else. My own voice.

And Beau's.

"Go," the cat commanded.

I tried. Something wasn't right. I couldn't put my finger on what. I didn't have any fingers. *That must be it.* I didn't have any hands or feet either.

How can I go anywhere without hands or feet?

The house seemed so far away.

I have to get to the house.

I have to get back to my body.

16

Returning to myself turned out to be as simple as thinking those words. One second I was outside, in the road, barely able to form coherent thoughts, the next, my consciousness snapped into place.

My consciousness had come back but without awareness of my surroundings. My head went crashing into the scrying bowl, splashing water everywhere. I jerked up, showering the walls and window.

My head and my hair were drenched—something I'd usually curse about. But then, I couldn't have cared less. I was just happy to be whole again. I knew in the pit of my stomach that I'd come awfully close to losing myself— freeing my spirit to wander off. Perhaps for eternity. Or at least until Aunt Cora reined me in.

Hearing the commotion, Ingrid rapped lightly on the open doorway. "You all right?" She poked her head in the room. A look of amusement crossed her face. "Let me get you a towel."

She was gone a second, then returned and tossed a hand towel across the room.

"Thanks." I dabbed my forehead dry.

"Was that your first time scrying?"

"Is it that obvious?" I returned her amused smile with one of my own.

Behind Ingrid, the cat rounded the corner into the bedroom. "I was trying to warn you *not* to do that," Cora hissed.

"I'll make sure to listen next time." Not that there was going to be a next time. No. Scrying was worse than visions. And I still didn't understand its purpose. All I'd accomplished was nearly ending everything.

Cora, or the cat, wound around Ingrid's leg. "Now," she said, "tell us what you saw out there."

"I don't know." What had I seen? I tried to reconstruct the memories, but the memories weren't really there. They were like cardboard cutouts of memories. "Let's see. I went through the wall. And I was floating there. Then I thought I'd ride the breeze."

"Silly girl. You're lucky you didn't blow across the state. Or worse."

"What would be worse?"

"Never mind that. You aren't planning to do it again, are you?"

"Scrying?" I asked. "Definitely not."

"Not scrying—*going outside*," she stressed. "As long as you stay in this house, you can scry all you want."

"I think I'd rather not. You know. Just to be safe." With the towel, I sopped up the water left on the desk. "What's even the point? I didn't see anything out there that I wouldn't have had I—" I stopped, realizing those words weren't true.

"It's like I told you before," Cora said. "Scrying isn't like soul searching. It *is* soul searching. It splits the you of your mind from the you of your soul."

"But what's the point of it?"

Aunt Cora hopped onto my lap and onto the desk. She skirted the remnants of water. We were now at eye level, and her yellow eyes bored into mine. "It allows you to see things you'd never see through your mind's eye—you'd never see them *because* of your mind's eye!"

"Okay..."

"It's a powerful thing to relive the past. To slip back into your old life. Or slip into the future. Your soul is eternal. Your body is not. It's this special connection—this bond with our soul that others call our third eye."

Ingrid leaned on the doorjamb. She looked bored, as if she'd heard it all before.

I, on the other hand, hung on every word, mesmerized by this new information.

The cat prowled around the table, as if Cora was pacing. "It has other uses as well. Uses you might be inclined to try should you continue your investigative pursuits. When scrying, you're all but invisible to the world."

"Except here," I said. "What kind of spell makes a soul solid?"

"It's nothing to concern yourself over. It came in handy from time to time. Sometimes, I'd forget which was which. I did several readings in my spirit form. No one was the wiser."

"The two bodies wouldn't tip them off?"

"I used this bowl upstairs. The one downstairs is for show. I'd never leave my body when using it."

"Good to know."

"Scrying's actually what facilitated this." Aunt Cora bobbed the head of the cat around, picked up a paw, then the other. "It helps I knew the exact time of my body's death down to the second. I slipped out, left my body behind with my head resting in my hands—as I always did. But instead of staying in place above the bowl, my hands folded. My head slumped into the scrying bowl. Just like yours did."

"So, you drowned?"

"Were you listening, child? I was already dead. My body went limp. It's irrelevant where my face went after that."

"If it was irrelevant, then why'd you say it?"

"I was painting the picture."

"I didn't need it painted," I told her. "In fact, I had a vision of your death."

"You thought I was going to drown, and you didn't have the decency to call me?"

That wasn't fair. "I tried. I called. It rang and rang." It wasn't a lie. Granted, I could've tried a lot harder.

Neither Aunt Cora nor Ingrid offered a response.

"I'm sorry," I said.

"I'm just messing with you." Aunt Cora nudged my hand with her head. "I missed that call on purpose. I never liked goodbyes. And I knew I was going to do this."

"Why this though? Couldn't you have stayed a soul, like I did?"

"I could have. But it would've been a lot harder to hide when I needed to hide. Hard to explain to folks if they saw me as me. And like you saw firsthand, it's much harder for spirits when they're out of the house. As the cat, I can go where I please."

I nodded in understanding. Then I remembered. "You saved me. When I was in the road. You saved me."

"You saved yourself," she said.

"But you're right. If you hadn't been out there, I don't know what would've happened. I..."

There had been more than a cat in that grass. Two children playing. Me and Beau.

"That's it. I did see something out there. Just like you said."

"What?" Both Cora and Ingrid asked.

"Me and Beau," I said.

"What do you think it means?" Ingrid was the one to ask.

"I think it means I've been afraid to see him. If I'm going to solve this murder—whether he was involved with it or not—I've got to talk to him. I don't think I was ready to until now."

IT TOOK the better part of the afternoon and the leveraging of several local connections to set up a visit for the next day. I made calls to the county jail, had a short conversation with Mrs. Kenner at Artemis Green's office, and finally called my cousin Josh, who helped smooth things over.

Josh was a deputy in the county sheriff's department. But more importantly, he knew people. Lots and lots of people. The problem was now he knew I was in town, which meant my whole extended family would too. They were sure to come out of the woodwork just as Aunt Cora's former clients had lined up at her door.

The jail was about fifteen minutes north of the interstate, down a secluded stretch of road, well off the beaten path. There wasn't anything remarkable about it. Like most county jails, it boasted a menacing amount of razor wire fencing surrounding a blocky concrete structure that was anything but inviting.

I went through the usual protocols, handed over my identification, and got thoroughly searched on my way inside. It wasn't until I was ushered into the next room that I learned Beau had other visitors that day.

Beau's mother and his sister Alaina were waiting to see him. They looked both surprised and relieved to see me.

"Willow." Mrs. King got to her feet. "Does this mean you've found something?"

"Mom!" Alaina threw an elbow at her mother.

"What?" Mrs. King glared at her daughter. "She's here, isn't she? It has to mean something."

"That's right," Alaina argued. "She's here. Isn't that enough? You really think she's solved the case in a couple of days—when it took the real police months to even bring Beau in for questioning?"

The real police, I thought snidely. *Yeah, right.*

"You're a life saver," Alaina said to me. "I'm glad you changed your mind about Beau, even if you won't give us a reading."

At that remark, Mrs. King rolled her eyes.

"That's not what I do. This is."

The older woman appreciated the sentiment. She took my hand in hers. "Tell us what you've learned so far."

The edges of my vision clouded with tendrils of white.

Suddenly, I was driving down Highway 83.

No, I wasn't driving. The hands on the steering wheel weren't mine. The skin was looser, the veins more prominent. These were Mrs. King's hands—the same hands that were holding mine.

She gripped the steering wheel like it might run away from her. But her old Lincoln was a smooth ride. It barreled past Mr. Thomas's truck on the side of the road.

He waved.

And the tension of visiting Beau poured out of her. She

wanted him home. She blamed herself, for firing him from the factory. She blamed herself for a lot of things.

She took a deep breath and smiled over at Alaina in the passenger seat. *My girl*, she thought sadly. *My girl is lying to me.*

"Tell me again," she said, "why do you need the money?"

"Momma," Alaina huffed, "we've been over it already. It's a loan. I'll pay you back. We'll pay you back."

"I understand what a loan is. I'm asking why you need it."

"You wouldn't understand. It's for some business expenses—"

"I run a business," Mrs. King protested.

"You manage a business," Alaina argued. "This is different. It's nothing. A new chair. Some random supplies. Forget it. Forget I ever mentioned it."

"I'll give you the loan." Her head was still tilted toward the passenger seat. Her eyes were half on the road but mostly on Alaina.

"Watch out!" Alaina cried.

Mrs. King's attention went to the road ahead where a giant snapping turtle was leisurely crossing the lane. She hit the brakes and swerved, narrowly avoiding the creature, only for the tires to find some debris on the shoulder.

That smooth steering seized beneath her grip. The back right tire made a flap-flapping sound with every spin.

A flat.

"Willow, are you all right?" Mrs. King jerked me away from the vision.

"Yeah," I said, blinking. "I am. I'm sorry. What were you saying?"

It was hard to judge how many people had seen what happened. Both Mrs. King and Alaina were staring.

"What was that?" Alaina squinted, studying my eyes. She'd seen them cloud over.

"Blood sugar," I lied. "I really should've eaten before I came."

"I might have a Snickers bar in my purse," Mrs. King dug around in her purse and held out the candy.

"I thought you said you didn't have any food."

"As I recall, I asked you if it was an emergency, and you said it wasn't."

"This isn't either." I waved it off. But she wasn't having it. I ended up with a Snickers in my hand. I smiled. "Again, I'm sorry. What were you asking me before?"

"I asked what you'd learned so far. Do you have any theories? Any leads?"

"I'm afraid I don't," I told her.

She frowned.

"If it makes you feel better, I'm still asking questions. It's why I'm here. I've got to ask Beau a few things."

"It does help." Alaina stepped in. "Momma, you go talk to Beau. We'll go in one at a time. How 'bout that?"

"Are you sure?" her mother asked.

I shook my head. "I can stay out here. Y'all go."

"No," Alaina insisted. "Let her go. I'll stay out here with you and keep you company."

Mrs. King and a few others were led back, leaving me in the cramped waiting area with Alaina and a guard.

We sat down, and I split the Snickers in half. "Here you go."

She took the candy.

After that vision, I had questions for her—questions I didn't know how to ask. The trouble was, she was chewing something too. And it wasn't just the nougat topped with caramel, peanuts, and chocolate.

Alaina gathered up the courage. "That was a vision, wasn't it?"

My reaction told her everything she needed to know. I tried to head her off. "What are you talking about?"

"You're the real deal—just like Cora said. I never saw a vision live and in person like that. But I heard things about Cora. Supposedly, her eyes went all white like that too."

"You weren't supposed to see that."

"It happened in the parlor too," she said. "A blink of the eye—I almost missed it. I thought it was a trick of the light."

"You saw that too." I took a comforting bite of the candy bar.

What's Aunt Cora going to say about this?

"I guess you aren't going to tell me what you saw." Alaina waited for my response.

I can lie to her now, but what good would it do?

"Y'all are going to get a flat tire on the way home." I balled up the wrapper in my hands.

"And before, at the parlor?"

"Shawna was going to trip on the porch. I stopped her."

"That's it?"

"That's it." I sent the trash flying for the waste bin.

The guard raised both hands like I'd shot a three pointer from downtown. I noticed that his attention was more focused on Alaina.

"That's it," I said. "That's the extent of my psychic abilities."

"I think you're being modest. Shawna thinks you're a fraud."

"She does?"

Alaina nodded. "To be honest, I was surprised she wanted to come with me the other day. She'd started to treat that place like my momma does."

"Why?"

Alaina leaned toward me, whispering, "I hate to speak ill of the dead."

"Aunt Cora?"

She nodded again. "In the months before she died, Cora wasn't acting right." Alaina peered around the waiting room like someone might be eavesdropping. The guard by the door was still looking at her. Alaina pressed on anyway. "When it came to consultations, Cora was always brutally honest. Mystical but honest. This was different. Some folks liked it. It was like she was being straight with them for the first time. But lots of folks, they stopped going altogether. They went elsewhere."

"Like Shawna?"

"Like Shawna." She sighed.

"Not you?"

"Oh, no. I was the other sort." She shrugged. "I liked it. I never went in for that mystical hoo-ha. You know—her talking in circles about energies and opening myself up to new opportunities. This was straight talk. Practical stuff. Well worth my money."

"Speaking of money, I understand you need a loan?"

"How do you—" Alaina's eyes went wide. "Oh. You really did see us getting a flat tire. I mean I believed you. But I didn't. You know?"

"I get it," I said. "Sometimes I don't believe it myself. What do you need that money for, Alaina?"

"Well, it's nothing bad—if that's what you think."

"What's it for? You can tell me."

"It's actually because of my last consult with Cora. Willow, you can't tell anyone—especially my momma."

"Spit it out," I said, almost laughing.

"Fine. Okay. I'm going out on my own. There's a space

opening up beside Sabal's. I put down a deposit on it. And I need to come up with the rest of the money... soon."

"Wow," I said. "Does Shawna know?"

She shook her vehemently. I couldn't tell if it was because of Shawna or because Mrs. King had walked through the door.

"Alaina, do you want to speak to your brother?"

"I do," she said. She turned to me. "I'll be quick. Promise."

Mrs. King took her seat. "You gave her some of that Snickers. You are too kind, Willow Brown. Too kind. I told Beau you're here."

"How'd he take that?"

"About as I'd expect."

I had no clue what that meant, but it wasn't that important. Something else was. "Mrs. King, can I ask you something?"

"I'm here," she said. "And you're already asking, so I guess so."

"What happened between you and Aunt Cora?"

Mrs. King raised an eyebrow. "Cora never told you?"

"It might come as a surprise to you, but I didn't really get on with Aunt Cora that well. Her leaving her house to me came as quite a shock."

"That sounds like her. She cared more about the shock value—the drama of it all—than for the person sitting in the seat beside her. Take my words to heart, should you ever decide to fill her role."

"I assure you I will." I also assured myself I'd never fill Cora's shoes in that parlor.

"I went to Cora for a reading," Mrs. King started. "Something happened. Something like what just happened with you. Cora's eyes filled with smoke. She tried to play it off—

also like you. Tried to tell me I was in some sort of grave peril. But wouldn't tell me how. Not really. Not until I pressed harder."

"And?"

"And she agreed to tell me—if I never came back to see her again. That was it."

"What'd she tell you?"

"There was going to be an accident at the factory. A fire. It wasn't going to be my fault. But I wasn't supposed to make it out alive."

"There wasn't a fire?"

"Oh, there was a fire. I just happened to be right there with a fire extinguisher. I was the hero, for a day. Afterward, everyone forgot.

"I guess you could say I resented it. I resented Cora for being right. I resented everyone else for not seeing what it could've been." Mrs. King patted my hand. When nothing happened, I let out a sigh of relief. "It's a funny way to repay the person who saved your life, isn't it? I never spoke to Cora again. You tell her I'm grateful—should you ever talk to her. All right?"

I squeezed her hand. "I will."

Alaina emerged from the doorway. The guard winked at her, and she blushed.

"You're up," Alaina said. "He's excited to see you."

"Thank you," Mrs. King said. I didn't know for what.

But when I got to the door, I remembered something. "Mrs. King," I called. "Watch out for turtles on the way home."

"Turtles?" She scowled.

"Turtles," Alaina repeated, helping her mother out of the chair. "We'll be on the lookout."

17

There was so much of the boy I once knew in the man that Beau Robinson had become. They had the same wide smile, a dimple in each cheek. The same deep set dark eyes were hidden behind rectangular glasses—like they had been since third grade.

But the differences overshadowed the similarities. Beau was bigger than I remembered, taller, with thick muscles. His head was completely shaved. He had tattoos down the length of his left arm and a few on his right.

"You don't have to say it." Beau's smile somehow grew wider. "Khaki is not my color." He waved up and down, gesturing from his shoes to his shirt. "I know it. They know it. But it's what they pick out for me every morning—like they're my momma back in elementary school."

"You always said you dressed yourself."

"I did. I put my own clothes on, one leg at a time. She just picked 'em out. I hated going over to the mall. An hour each way for clothes—and she'd never let me go in the record store or the arcade."

"Poor Beau," I said. "Alaina always claimed you got babied when I wasn't around."

"And look who gets babied now." He folded his arms over his chest and rolled his eyes. "I swear, that girl gets away with murder." He winced. "Probably not the best turn of phrase for me to use."

"Probably not," I agreed. "How are you?"

"Honestly, Wills, I've been better."

I'd completely forgotten about that nickname—Wills. Tim didn't even have a nickname for me, other than baby, sugar, or sweetheart.

"Your momma tell you why I'm here?"

"She mentioned it," he said. "She also told me why you're here in Florida. I bet you're thrilled to get that place in your name." There was sarcasm dripping from his voice.

"You know me." I realized he did know me, at least an older version.

It was jarring to hear Beau speak to me like Nikki—like my best friend. Like there wasn't twenty-some years and the plexiglass between us.

"Madam Willow's. I don't think that has the right ring to it."

"Me either."

"How bad is it?" He frowned. "You know if I was out of here, I'd help you fix it up. That's what I do now—fix up houses. Handyman stuff. I don't know if you heard."

"I've heard a lot of things." There was a hint of derision in my voice.

He tried to change the subject. "Remember when we kissed?"

It wasn't going to work. "Nope. I blocked that from my memory ages ago."

"Why? It was a good kiss."

I was incredulous. Maybe it *was* going to work. "A good kiss? No. I heard you tell one of your friends that I had the most rank breath you'd ever smelled."

Beau looked stunned. "Wait. You heard that?"

I nodded.

"It was Chris, right? I told Chris that."

"Does it matter who?" I asked him.

"It does kinda matter." His brown eyes were as fascinating as they were when we were kids. I wanted to look away, but I was captured. "Chris had a huge crush on you. I was afraid if I told him you were a good kisser, he'd try to find out for himself."

My jaw went slack.

"If I remember correctly," he continued, "you told me the next week that you were moving. And you were happy because you'd never have to see my dumb face again. I guess that sums it up, right?"

"It does," I agreed. "Now, we both sound dumb."

"So dumb." He smiled. "I'm glad to see your dumb face again—in spite of the circumstances."

"Same." We came down to Earth. "Now, tell me in your own words why you're here."

He leaned his chair on its back legs. "A misunderstanding."

"What's that supposed to mean, Beau?"

He sighed. "It means things are more complicated than they look. I can't really talk about it right now."

"Beau," I scolded him, "this is your chance to clear the air—to tell your side of the story, like you did about the kiss. I'm here today. Gone, not tomorrow, but soon." I wished it was tomorrow. I'd still be in Mossy Pointe for a few more days at least.

He bent his chin to his chest and studied his hands. "What do you want to know?"

"Start at the beginning. What happened that day?"

"Nothing much," he said. "I did some work for Alaina. I left. I went down to the river and took out my boat for a while, did some fishing. I came back to town later and I heard about Perry. That's it."

"You took out your boat? Did anyone see you do that?"

"Maybe." He shrugged. "Maybe not."

"That's helpful."

"What do you want me to say?"

"The truth."

"I'm telling you the truth," he protested.

"If you are, it's just part of it. A version with something left out. Why'd you turn off your phone? How much money did you owe Perry?"

"You won't like the answers to those questions."

"How much?"

"Let's say a lot."

"And the phone?"

He brushed his face with a hand. "I have a question for you."

"I'm listening."

"If I asked you to stay out of this, would you?"

I considered. "Probably. Does that mean you did it?"

"No, Wills. It does not mean I did it. You have to understand I had nothing to do with Perry's murder."

"But?"

"But there's other things going on. Other people. I don't want you involved."

"I'm already involved."

He shook his head. "Okay. Here it is. Hypothetically, I owed this person a large sum of money. And through a friend of a friend of a friend, I knew how to make a large sum of money, just for driving my boat from one end of the river to the other."

"Drugs?"

"Why don't you say it a little louder? I don't think the guard heard."

"Beau!"

He held up his hand. "I don't need a lecture. What I need is for you to understand why I can't give these people up. They have people in here. People out. I can't exactly say what I was really doing during the time my phone was off. You get that, right?"

"I get it. Who are they?"

"They're called the Swamp Ghosts."

"Cool name."

"I know, right?"

"What can I do?" I asked.

"Nothing."

"That's not true. I could find the *real* killer."

"The cops already tried that."

"Do you think this gang—the Swamp Ghosts—have any connection to Perry?"

He shrugged. "I can't say for sure. It's possible. He was throwing some serious money around before he died. But Wills, I really don't want you to go near those people."

"Then give me someone else."

For a second, he held his mouth open, and I thought he might. He closed it.

If I wanted to learn any more about this gang, I'd have to ask Chief Hammonds when I went over to his house for dinner.

18

The Hammonds lived at the end of their street, in a cul-de-sac. Their house was the lone new one in a sea of older homes. It was nice but not fancy.

I brought along dessert, a Key lime pie I'd commandeered from Henry.

I'd stopped at Sabal's Grill on the way home, happy not to see Mrs. King stranded on the side of the road on my way back from the jail.

After an hour or so of gossip with Nikki, I was running late. I made a hurried call to Tim before rushing off to this soiree.

That was Nikki's joke. It wasn't a soiree, not in the slightest. But the word had stuck in my head.

Chief Hammonds opened the door, still in his ratty uniform. "Honey, she's here," he called. "We weren't sure you'd make it."

Where else did I have to go? Nowhere but Cora's with the talking cat and the strange roommate.

"You didn't think she'd make it," said a female voice from inside the house. "I, on the other hand, had faith." A middle-aged blonde appeared beside him. She exuded a Stepford vibe, although that could've been the frilly white apron. "You need to get changed, mister." She patted her husband on the tush.

"Fine. Fine. Kit, this is Willow. Willow, Kit."

I put my hand out to shake hers, but she was a hugger. She brought her arms around me and I stood there like a fish out of water. "I'm Katherine but everyone calls me Kit or Kitty."

"Kitty? Like a cat."

"Exactly." She made claws. "Meow."

Kit cringed at her own joke—or maybe I cringed and she mirrored it. "I don't know why I did that," she said. "Please. Don't think I'm weird. I don't get out much. I'm constantly surrounded by children."

There were no children I could see and no sound other than faint beach music coming from a stereo. We went into a great room, and there were still no signs of life. No toys or highchairs.

"Oh, I should clarify. I work at a school. We haven't had children." By the tone of her voice and her expression, I had an idea of what she meant.

My Stepford judgment was harsh and premature. I had an unwritten kinship with this woman.

I wasn't ready to open up to her yet. For that, I'd need a lot of wine.

There was an open bottle on the massive kitchen island, next to a charcuterie board of fruits and cheeses.

"What do you teach?" I asked her.

"I'm the principal. But kind of like Ken's job, it mostly means I'm the first substitute. I was subbing in Mrs. Richards's first grade class this week."

"Wait. Mrs. Richards is still there?"

"A dilemma," Kit said. "She turned eighty-three this year and doesn't plan on retiring anytime soon."

She took two glasses down from the cupboard. "Could I interest you in a glass of wine?"

"That sounds lovely."

"Oh, and I wasn't sure if you were a vegetarian? I normally put out some cold cuts with this too."

"I'm mostly carnivore actually." I grinned.

With a wineglass in each hand, she let out a deep sigh of relief. "That's so good. I didn't know what we'd do for dinner if you were. Grill mushrooms or something. The reason I ask is our last guest was."

"The chief mentioned you like entertaining."

Kit handed me a glass, then went to the fridge and began pulling out meats, making rolls of several kinds. It made the colorful board even more appealing. But also made me reluctant to mess up its beauty.

"I love having people over," she said. "It's difficult here. The town is so small. I don't meet many people outside of school and church."

"We've hosted a few dinner parties." Chief Hammonds had changed into jeans and a polo. They weren't as ill-fitting as his uniform but still had the appearance of belonging to a man who'd recently lost some weight.

The chief wasn't nearly as worried about the beauty of the board. He dented it badly in a matter of minutes.

Finally, I was comfortable enough to join him.

"That's true," Kit agreed. "A few means three, right? When we were in Atlanta, we had a party every month. Sometimes more than one."

"It's different here," he said.

"It doesn't have to be." Kit took a beer from the fridge and handed it to him.

"I know. I know." Beer in one hand, he put the other up placatingly. "I've got to put myself out there more. And I will after this case is resolved. I promise."

"That could be years if it goes to trial." I took a cluster of grapes and popped a couple in my mouth.

"It won't," he said, a shade of gruffness in his voice. "The prosecutor's offering a plea deal. Marge assured me it's a matter of time until Beau agrees to it."

"He won't agree to it."

"No? Why not?"

"Because he didn't do it." For the first time since stepping into this whole mess, I let my opinion be heard.

I probably shouldn't have voiced it to the chief of police. There was no backing down now. I had to solve this case.

"Can you tell me what you know about the Swamp Ghosts? Could Perry have fallen in with them? Crossed the wrong person?"

"Like I told you at my office—I don't really deal with the drug stuff. That's the county's jurisdiction. Doesn't your cousin work out there?"

"He does. But I'm asking you—did your investigation include them?"

The chief took a swig of beer and didn't reply.

Kit was happy to jump in. "Ken, how about you get the grill started? Willow and I are fine in here." She refilled my glass.

A little while later, Ken brought in a pork tenderloin and let it rest while he finished grilling some vegetables. I was surprised to see cheese grits and grilled bread as the offered carbohydrates.

We dug in and chatted a while. I answered several questions about my marriage that made me uncomfortable and dodged several more.

Ken and Kit were a lovely couple. How they'd ended up in Mossy Pointe was beyond me. So, I asked.

"It's not much of a story really," Ken started. "We wanted to find a small town to settle in. So, we both started job searching, sending out resumes, that kind of thing. We both got a few offers elsewhere but never the same place."

"Except here," Kit added. "It was meant to be."

"Is it permanent?" I asked.

"That's a funny question." Kit considered. "I don't know. Ken?"

"I don't know either." He turned to me. "I'm sorry about before. This case has me on edge. I understand you and Beau were close growing up. I'm real sorry things are the way they are."

"I get it." I understood more than most where he was coming from. "I'm sorry if I'm unconvinced."

He shrugged. "I have a few copies of Beau's book if you want to take a peek."

"Sure."

"Oh, you two." Kit smiled. "I'll slice that pie while you do your police business."

Chief Hammonds took me to a study, much tidier than his office. There was just a computer and a stack of manila folders on the desk.

There was a photo sticking out of the top folder. It took me a second to realize what I was looking at—who I was looking at.

The picture was of Ingrid.

Without thinking, I held in a breath.

"I'm sure you can understand—sometimes I bring my work home with me." The chief handed me the second folder from the stack.

I gave it the briefest of glances. The handwriting was familiar enough.

My one-track mind was on that photo.

I set down the folder beside the computer and nudged the other. "Who's she?" I knew the answer. Or I thought I did.

I wanted to peek into the file and see what it said. I didn't need to see Beau's ledger to know he'd been gambling with Perry.

The chief picked up the photo and shook his head sadly. "Well, her name is Ingrid."

Check.

He went on, "It would be your standard missing persons case except—"

"Except we know her." Kit was at the door with slices of pie on dessert plates.

"Knew her," the chief said. "She passed through town, what, about a year ago?" He took his plate and nodded at his wife to continue.

"Ten months," she said. "I'm still holding on to some hope. But it's not looking good, is it?"

I struggled to process their meaning and completely disregarded the plate Kit tried to hand me.

As far as I knew, Ingrid was at Cora's house, and she was fine. She wasn't missing. "Tell me again, how you know Ingrid?"

"Like I said, about ten months ago Ingrid was passing through town, staying at the Inn. Kitty ran into her at the grocery store." The chief took a bite of pie and motioned with a fork.

His wife jumped in. "We struck up a conversation. I invited her over. We had a dinner much like this one. Except she was a vegetarian. Luckily, I kind of noticed when I saw her cart at the store."

"And?" I asked. "What happened after that?"

"That was it." The chief shrugged. "There wasn't much to it. Not until about two weeks later. Deputies found a car abandoned down 83, near the river. They ran the plates. It was Ingrid's car. From the looks of it, she ran out of gas and was walking down the highway."

"And she disappeared?"

He nodded. "I helped search. We contacted her family—who said what we already knew—she was a college dropout who wanted to be a writer. Her father had left her a little money, and she set out, on the road like Jack Kerouac."

"Which is funny because she'd never read *On the Road*," Kit said. "I lent her my copy."

"They found it in her car. The pages were bent up."

"Like that matters," Kit said. "I prefer my books to be loved."

The chief tucked Ingrid's picture into the folder and closed it. "The deputies got her last known number and tried calling it. No answer. We don't have anything to go on."

I wanted to tell them they were wrong. That I knew where Ingrid was this very minute. But something inside me told me not to say a word. If she went missing—if she disappeared like that—she probably had a good reason.

Murder was a good reason to disappear. But the timeframe wasn't lining up.

"You said she disappeared ten months ago? So, this was before Perry's murder."

"Yes," the chief said. "It was a couple months before that."

Okay. That was a good thing. Maybe Ingrid wasn't a

murderer. Maybe she had another good reason to lay low. I could at least hear her out before exposing her existence.

"Do you suspect foul play?"

"I, uh," he wavered. "The car was abandoned; there were no signs of a struggle. The county took point on this case. They did their due diligence—checked the local hospitals and all that."

"I really hope she's found," Kit said. "She was a sweet girl."

"I do too." The chief pressed his lips together and turned to me. "If I'm honest, I do think foul play. Maybe those Swamp Ghosts. Maybe someone else. It's not my investigation."

"So, where is she?" I asked.

"I don't believe she's with us any longer, not in the mortal world."

The mortal world.

The reality of my situation hit me square in the chest. Ingrid wasn't a roommate in the true sense of the word. She was a ghost.

19

"**I**ngrid!" I called into the empty house. "Cora!"

No answer.

"I'd like to speak to both of you in the parlor." I slammed the front door shut, hoping to emphasize my point.

I was angry. I was confused. I'd been lied to.

That's how I felt. Then again, there were other ways I could look at it. Out of the three of us, this revelation about Ingrid meant the least for me. I wasn't dead or dying. If anything, Ingrid being a ghost made things easier. She was no longer in the way of selling the house. She never had been.

As soon as I flicked on a lamp, Ingrid appeared, seated at the table. I didn't even flinch. My mind had already come to terms with the situation. I'd been living with a ghost for two days.

A moment later, the gray cat sauntered into the room. She leaped nimbly onto the table next to the purple phone and the crystal ball. "You rang?"

I shook my head, clenching and unclenching my jaw. I

wasn't mad at Ingrid. But I could still be angry with Cora. "Why wouldn't you tell me Ingrid is a ghost?"

"Who said I wouldn't?"

"You never did."

"You never asked." The cat licked a paw, solidifying her position—unimpressed with my little tantrum.

I pressed the point. "Why would I ask a question like that? She told me she was your roommate."

"In a way, she is."

"I'm a ghost?" Ingrid pinched her forearm, then touched her cheeks. "Are you sure? I don't feel like a ghost."

"What happens to you if you go outside?" I asked.

"I'm not allowed out," she said. "House rules."

I rubbed my temples. "You're a ghost."

"But I'm real. I'm solid. See?" She poked me.

For a brief moment, I was no longer in the room. That touch propelled me straight into a vision in a way no other touch ever had.

But all I saw were headlights. They were so bright. Blinding me. And it was over. I was back in the dimly lit parlor.

"You aren't really solid, dear," Cora said. "You remember Willow's scrying?"

"Oh, yeah." She patted down her dark hair. "I am a ghost, aren't I?"

"You're lucky I called you here," Cora said.

"What do you mean you called her?"

The cat tilted its head. "I sensed her spirit wandering nearby. So, I called it here—her here. And I offered her the house's protection."

"Why though? Why would you?"

"Because she was lost," Cora said. "There's nothing

worse than a spirit lost in the afterlife. Imagine it—wandering alone for eternity."

"I get it." I tried not to imagine it. There was no telling how many spirits ended up in that state. And no answers to *why*. Or rather, no answers I was privy to.

"You don't," Cora argued. "But that's a lesson for another time."

"Do you know how she died?" I asked. "Ingrid, do you know how you died?"

"I'm afraid not," Cora said.

I remembered those blinding headlights. *Is it really that simple?*

"Was it a car accident?" I asked. "Ingrid, do you remember? Do you know how you ended up here?"

"I was walking down the road," she said. "Then I... then I was at the door. Cora answered."

"But you don't remember before that? What about your car? What happened to it?"

"Oh, my car. I do remember. It was yellow. It ran out of gas. I'd never run out of gas before. It felt silly. Stupid, even. My phone couldn't get a signal. I thought I would walk and find a signal. I started walking and..."

Pausing, she smiled at her own reflection in the crystal ball on the table. I hoped she would keep going, try to recover the memories between leaving the car and becoming a spirit.

No such luck.

Ingrid disappeared from the table. There was no sign of her anywhere in the room. At least, I didn't think so. Not until Aunt Cora tipped her head toward the crystal ball. Ingrid's reflection was still there, inside it.

"What happened to her?"

"She's still here," Cora answered. "She'll come back in

her own time. Reminding her that she's a ghost triggers a response. She has to want to be here. Asking her how she died is going to send her running the other way. For a ghost, that's the trauma we left—the memory of life."

"Can she still hear me?" I asked.

"She can."

"Ingrid. This is important. Do you know where your body is?"

With those words, her reflection in the crystal ball winked out.

"Now, look what you've done," Cora admonished.

"I'm trying to help her."

"False. You have your own agenda. If you cared about Ingrid—truly cared—you'd leave her be."

"You don't understand."

"What don't I understand?" The cat stalked across the table and sat facing me, eye to slitted yellow eyes. "You think her death is linked to the other murder. You're probably right. But this isn't the way to go about finding the answer. Choose another path, Willow."

I shook my head. "You were the one encouraging me to use my psychic abilities. Now you're saying I shouldn't?"

"Talking to a ghost is hardly a psychic ability," she hissed. "This is different. You're a sleuth. You have *other* skills. Use them."

I would've scoffed had those words not sparked an idea.

I might not've been in Mossy Pointe when Ingrid was killed. But I knew where to find a wealth of information from the time around her death.

Plus, I knew something the local police didn't—information that would turn Perry's murder investigation on its head.

Ingrid wasn't missing. She was deceased. And whatever happened to her had led to Perry's murder.

I just had to figure out why.

———

From <u>Neighbor Sleuths</u> post Flashlights in the woods on Duck Pond Rd...

Kirk-JD: Anyone else hear voices or see flashlights down Duck Pond Rd last night?

StrangerThanFiction (Trusted User): What were you doing there? You don't even live down Duck Pond Rd, JD.

Kirk-JD: Bit of fishing. Bit of gigging. Not that it's any of your business.

Tooomz (Admin): I heard a car engine pretty late.

StrangerThanFiction (Trusted User): And what others do in the woods is yours?

Kirk-JD: Tooomz, it could've been mine.

Kirk-JD: Stranger, you're right. It's a free country. And that's county land. I was just afraid it might be riffraff of the ghost variety. It's too close to town for that nonsense.

Tooomz (Admin): It didn't sound like a Ford. No offense.

Kirk-JD: Well, I wouldn't have taken offense if you didn't say no offense. What's wrong with Ford?

StrangerThanFiction (Trusted User): Ah. Fair enough.

Tooomz (Admin): Besides the fact it's not a Dodge or a Chevy?

This conversation was archived by an admin.

20

"Hey, Josh, it's Willow."

"What do you want today?" On the other end of the line, my cousin sounded flustered. Granted, it was early, and I didn't know his work schedule. For all I knew, he was at the end of a graveyard shift.

"Are you working?" I asked.

"I'm about to go in."

Good. He was rested. His grumpy disposition had nothing to do with the timing, it was more to do with our familial relationship.

I, on the other hand, wasn't prepared for the usual give and take. I had a fitful night's sleep. Ingrid had never reappeared.

"What's this about?" he asked. "Beau again?"

"Not Beau. Not really. Listen. This isn't an easy thing to say. So, I'm just going to come out and say it. It'll be easier that way."

"Ta-ta-ta-ta-ta-today, cuz."

I hissed a sigh into the receiver. "Okay. I have good

reason to believe there's a body hidden at the end of Duck Pond Road."

The line went silent.

"You still there?"

"I'm here," he said. "A body—whose body?"

"A girl, a girl named Ingrid."

"Right." I could practically hear the gears whirring in his head. "Meet me out there in twenty."

I made it in ten.

Duck Pond Road ended abruptly at three reflective markers. The actual duck pond was a good hundred or more yards from the end of the road. A path gave easy access to people on foot. A dirt road ran along the other side of the pond and allowed vehicles to get to the dock and a boat ramp.

I waited for the cavalry to show up. But the cavalry was a lone sheriff's department cruiser with its lights off.

The car rolled to a stop behind mine. My second cousin, Josh Ramsey, stepped out.

Josh was an inch or two shorter than average and broad shouldered. He used to play linebacker on the football team, and it still showed; he was all neck and traps. His thighs were the size of tree trunks—redwoods.

"Is this it?" I asked. "Just you?"

"What'd you expect? Me to come rolling up with an excavator? I mean I do know a guy." He popped the trunk and pulled out an old shovel. He handed it to me, then reached in and grabbed another. "But the shovels are gonna have to do for now."

"No other deputies in the area? A detective or two?"

"You remember where you are, right?"

I sighed. This was going to be a lot harder than I thought. And I hadn't thought it was going to be easy.

The ground was mostly dirt and sand but with overgrown weeds and brambles in clumps. The grass, sprinkled here and there, was high. And there were bushes or stumps every few feet.

"If it makes you feel any better, I can get those folks. But there has to be a body. From the way you sounded on the phone, I wasn't so sure."

"Fair enough."

We started at the road, wading into the overgrown area, avoiding tripping hazards. There was a lot of ground to cover.

"I don't see any turned up dirt anywhere."

"It'd be six months old."

Josh adjusted his ball cap. He looked at me funny, squinting with skepticism. "Hold up a minute. This is some psychic bullcrap, isn't it?"

I gave him a slight shrug. "Maybe."

"You know, a while ago, you told me you weren't like my grandmamma."

"I might've lied."

"Yeah, well, I figured that much." He frowned, then shuddered. His eyes darted wildly. He wasn't scanning the landscape anymore; he was the checking the air around him. "Where is it? If there's a ghost around me, I want to know where it is. They make me uncomfortable."

"What makes you think there's a ghost around?"

"I know how this stuff works. She was my grandmamma." He checked over his shoulder, ducking like a bee had flown past his ear. "She's right behind me, isn't she?"

"She's not here."

"Good." He straightened. "Good."

"Okay. Now, she's right behind you." I could barely get

out the lie without laughing. Josh jumped away, grazing my arm in the process.

The edges of my vision went white.

It was too much. This town was too much. I couldn't think of a time I'd had this many visions in such a short span of time. I wanted to block this one—pretend I didn't care what might happen to Josh later that day.

But I did care.

I cared a lot.

Josh was returning to his squad car—late afternoon by the looks of the orange sky behind the vehicle.

His radio crackled. I listened to the dispatcher call out shots fired, and both me and Josh did a double take when she gave the address—2002 Main Street. Cora's house. My house.

I realized I should've blocked the vision out after all. It had nothing really to do with Josh.

It was about me. My fate.

I could run from it now. I could leave town and not come back.

But if I stayed, there was no telling if I was running to or away from it.

The vision ended.

Josh was still creeped out. Or maybe my vision had creeped him out further. He waggled a finger at me. "Don't be like that. This is serious business."

"You're right," I said. "I'm sorry."

"There's really no ghost here?"

"I'm sure."

"And you're sure her body's around here somewhere?"

"Not really."

"She didn't tell you? How'd she die, by the way?"

"She doesn't know."

"She doesn't know how she died or she doesn't know where her body is?"

"I've heard it both ways."

"Seriously?" With a huff, he plowed the shovel in the dirt. "Willow, what the heck are we doing out here then?"

"I have a theory. There was a post on *Neighbor Sleuths* around the time of her disappearance. Someone came out here that night with flashlights."

"So, you based your theory on *Neighbor Sleuths*? No. No —I can't take you seriously right now. The people on that site—they call the police if the wind blows the wrong direction. Everybody's a serial killer to them."

"Trust me," I coaxed. "I have good instincts."

"Like with Beau?"

"I've got several leads there too," I lied. "I think these cases are connected."

"Of course you do." Shovel in hand, he started toward a pine tree several yards ahead. "And what was your theory before that?"

I struggled to keep up. "You ever heard of the Swamp Ghosts?"

"Obviously. Local drug runners. They use the river. Is this them too?"

"I don't think so. But I am wondering, do you know any of them by name?"

"Uh, no. What part of ghost don't you get?" He stopped. "What a creepy coincidence. She still isn't here, right?"

"She's not."

"Okay. So, the Swamp Ghosts. You don't know any of them. But someone does, right?"

"Obviously *someone* knows. But they aren't going to talk to me. And I doubt they'd talk to you either. You look and smell like a cop."

"Look, I'll give you. But I smell about ten times better than you."

His eyes narrowed, and he strode off.

"What is it?" I followed his gaze, seeing nothing more than shrubs and loose sand.

"Hold on." He poked the tip of his shovel into the ground, carefully sifting through it. "I think we've got something here, Willow."

"What?"

"A body," he said, as if it were obvious.

"What? How?"

"Take a step back." He nudged me with an outstretched arm, then pointed. "Now, look here. What do you see?"

I saw dirt and weeds, nothing distinctive. I was looking too closely at the ground to see anything of value. But when I took another step back, I saw it—a slight mound that didn't quite make sense in the flat ground around it.

He moved weeds and sand before striking something more solid. Another few scoops of sand exposed a ribcage. "It's got to be her, right?"

I nodded.

"What do you think happened to her?"

"Like I said, she doesn't know. But I had this vision of headlights. I think it was some sort of car accident." I wished Ingrid had been able to give me more details. Or that I had been able to make out the car.

"An accident?" Josh scoffed. "You don't bury a body by accident."

"Agreed." Thinking about the car gave me an idea. A couple of ideas. "We should check the doorbell cameras and floodlights up the road. Maybe they'll have old footage."

Josh pursed his lips. "It's a good thought. Really, it is. But I'm guessing we'll run into the same issue we had with

Perry's murder. No one around here has them. And we'd be fighting an uphill battle if it was dark. Perry was murdered in broad daylight and they found a whole lot of nothing."

"I know. No one saw or heard anything. But I do have another idea."

"That is?"

"I'm thinking maybe Perry worked on this car. Did y'all happen to get records of whose cars he worked on in his garage at home?"

Josh shook his head. "Perry didn't keep records like that."

"Okay. I'm going to talk to Nikki and Henry then. Maybe they saw another car there when he worked on her Mustang."

"Good idea, but you can't go anywhere right now. When I call this in, they're gonna want to talk to you."

"I know," I said. "That's actually why I'd like to leave. I don't have that kind of time. I've got to solve this today."

"Why—what does that mean?"

I couldn't tell him about the future. I didn't know what it was. Not exactly. If that gun and those red fingernails from my dream were in it, then so be it.

I wasn't running away from them any longer.

21

J osh wasn't happy about me leaving, but I gave him little choice in the matter. He shook his head, pouting as I left him there, calling for backup.

I headed for Sabal's Grill. Nikki and Henry might not know any more than I did, but they were a good sounding board, and they'd back me up if things really went south.

Ingrid's death threw a wrench in the whole investigation —unless they weren't related.

They have to be.

Mossy Pointe was too small a town to draw any other conclusion. My gut said the Swamp Ghosts had to be part of this somehow.

But why would the Swamp Ghosts murder Ingrid? Should I exclude them, from Ingrid's murder at least?

And that was where I had to start. The beginning.

Ingrid had been missing for almost a year and nothing much happened. *Why?*

What had changed?

My mind was spinning. I had to do something to clear my head and sort out the jumbled thoughts.

I called my husband.

Tim answered on the second ring. He was driving too, road noise filling the speakers through my aftermarket Bluetooth connection. That made it hard to hear, and we were both yelling by the end.

"Love you."

"What?"

"I said, I love you," he yelled.

"I love you too."

I ended the call, my heart hammering, wondering if that was the last time I'd ever speak to my husband—over a poor connection, a thousand or so miles apart.

I made a pact with myself. This wasn't going to be the end. I was going to figure this out.

But I had to know who I was dealing with.

Sabal's Grill was hopping. There were a dozen people outside on benches waiting to get a seat. Every one of them gave me some side eye when I shouldered past. I muttered, "I'm meeting someone," and pushed through the door.

And sure enough, there were tables with people I knew. Not that any of them had plans with me.

Nikki wasn't at the hostess desk. The waitress from the other day was on the desk, and I didn't think she liked me. They were too busy for me to pull Nikki aside without a real explanation.

I couldn't exactly tell Nikki about Ingrid's ghost and finding her body—though the last part would be news soon enough. I scanned the sea of familiar faces. There had to be another way to get the information I needed.

A hand shot up. It waved.

The hand belonged to Shawna Grimes. Next to her, Alaina King smiled with her eyes as she sipped tea.

I gestured the universal "who, me?"

Shawna nodded and waved her manicured hand energetically.

I smiled and ventured over.

"Sit down with us," Shawna said. "We just got our drinks. Haven't even ordered yet."

My spot at the table, with the seat beside it, still had a menu and silverware.

"It's so busy," I said. "You're sure you have time to eat?"

"I took the afternoon off," Shawna said.

Alaina shrugged. "My next appointment's at one. I've got plenty of time. But you're right. No one misses barbecue day."

"That explains it." I nodded, flipping the menu over to the specials. It was strange to think the shed and the kitchen could've gone up in smoke had I not caused Nikki to spill coffee in Mr. Thomas's lap. "So, barbecue it is."

I set down the menu, seeing a Coke had materialized in front of me. There was still a hand attached to it.

"And a Coke," Nikki said. "Let me just say, this is not fair. You can't have a meeting of the minds without me."

"This is impromptu," I said. "And you look busy."

"I pay people for this. Let me bus a few tables and give Gertie my section. I'll be right over."

"With food?" Alaina asked skeptically.

"With food." Nikki winked.

Every second that passed was agonizing, but there was nothing I could do to hurry it up or stop it, either one. I had to roll with it.

We chatted about the salon for a few minutes. Alaina

might've stepped on my toes as I nearly broached the subject of her buying the space next door.

I guessed she wasn't telling Shawna until she had to. In my experience, partnerships—professional or otherwise—rarely weathered the kind of split she was proposing.

"Speaking of businesses," Shawna interrupted, "what's your plan for Madam Cora's? Are you ever opening it up?"

"That's not the plan. I have a few more loose ends to tie up, then I'm headed for Virginia."

Shawna nodded as if she'd been expecting that. "I get it."

"I don't," Nikki said, setting plates down, then scooting into the booth beside me.

"You don't?" Shawna looked surprised.

"And I really don't," Alaina cut in. "I know you have the gift."

It was my turn to step on her toes. "For the last time, I'm not a fortuneteller."

"Untrue," Nikki said. "You were always the best at cootie catchers and MASH."

"That's not fortunetelling." I laughed.

"It's not?" Nikki tilted her head, a smirk on her face.

"What?"

Shawna and Alaina were equally confused.

The vinyl seat groaned as Nikki scooted closer and leaned across the table conspiratorially. The rest of us leaned in to listen. She whispered, "What if I told you I still had the last MASH we did together? I was going through some old boxes, and I found our seventh-grade yearbook."

"I'd say you're nostalgic."

"Me too," Shawna agreed.

"No." Nikki shook her head, eyeing me with her deep brown eyes fringed with glorious lashes. "You'd say something like, 'Wow, Nikki. I really hit the nail on the head. Future husband: Henry. Number of kids: two. Future car: Mustang. Future City: Mossy Pointe—I remember putting that in as the place I *didn't* want to end up. And yet, here I am.'"

I rolled my eyes. "If I recall correctly, it was the same story for Henry."

Alaina started to giggle.

"Shhh!" Nikki put her finger to her mouth. "That's why I was whispering. He doesn't have to know he was my last choice. Granted, marrying Jonathan Taylor Thomas or Will Smith was kind of a stretch."

All four of us burst into laughter—which did draw Henry out of the kitchen. He scowled at Nikki, peered at his crowded restaurant, and shook his head.

"I better eat fast," she said. "And seriously, we need to have a girls' night before Willow leaves. I need out of the house. And out of town, preferably."

Alaina took a sip of tea and said, "There's a dive bar down near the coast Shawna likes."

"It's okay." Shawna shrugged. "But I'm down for whatever."

"Same," Nikki agreed.

"Yeah." I nodded as if I'd be anywhere near here after this afternoon.

We reminisced for a while. It never felt like the right time to bring up Perry. Or Beau.

Close to an hour passed and the lunch rush was winding down. I didn't know how much longer I had, but it couldn't be long.

My eyes started following our waitress around the dining room. And I wasn't the only antsy one at the table. Shawna kept looking toward the cash register. "I've got some cash," she said finally. "I'm going to leave this here. I've got to get going."

"Have a nice afternoon off," Alaina said, teasing. "Hope it's as relaxing as mine is taxing."

"Oh, I don't know about that." Shawna gathered her red purse and car keys. She started to leave, then stopped and said, "I almost forgot to ask—you've got a ride this afternoon, right?"

"I do." Alaina nodded.

"Good. I'm glad. Girl, I'm tired of driving you around everywhere."

"You *still* haven't got a new car?" Nikki's brow furrowed.

"Not yet. I haven't found anything I like for the right price."

"What's the right price?" Nikki asked.

"Cheap," Shawna said.

"Not cheap," Alaina disagreed. "Inexpensive."

"Whatever you say." Shawna waved goodbye and headed for the door.

I dipped a cold fry in ketchup.

"I still can't believe you up and sold your Camaro." Nikki shook her head mournfully. "We were like the muscle car queens up until then. A Dodge Challenger, a Chevy Camaro, and a Ford Mustang. All we needed was Willow to get a Firebird."

"Yeah, right." I rolled my eyes.

Nikki disregarded me. "A year is a long time to be without a car."

I almost choked on the French fry. "When was that?" I coughed.

"When was what?" Alaina asked.

"Your car—you sold it a year ago?"

"Almost, I guess." She shrugged. "Why?"

"No reason." I cleared my throat and drank the rest of my Coke, trying to regain my composure.

Alaina saw her opportunity to leave. "Yeah, well, I guess I better go too—in case my appointment gets there early. You know how these ladies are. You can't make them wait."

"That's for sure," Nikki agreed.

We watched her go.

I was too stunned to say much of anything. I pushed my basket to the center of the table.

"You're gonna leave me too? Make me go back to work?"

"Actually, I have a question for you."

"Shoot."

"Is the place next door for sale?"

"It used to be. I'm not sure if it still is. You could ask Marge. She'd know."

"I think maybe I will." But I didn't really want to go alone. "Nikki, would it be possible for you to come with me?"

She straightened, peering at the kitchen doors. "I'm already in hot water here."

"Oh. All right. No worries."

"That was a yes." A mischievous grin spread across her face. "I'm already in hot water. It can't get much hotter."

Time would tell if she was right.

22

"Ah, Miss Brown. You've brought the paperwork?" Mrs. Kenner stood and came around her desk to meet us.

"It's missus," I reminded her. A pang of guilt shot through my chest. I had to make some time to call Tim again. I had to. As long as I did it before I went back to Cora's house, it would be all right, I rationalized.

Everything's going to be all right, I thought. But another voice in my head said I was lying to myself.

The law office of Artemis Green took up the second story of the building. They'd rented out the first floor to a dance studio—Kenner's School of Ballet and Tap that I assumed was run by Mrs. Kenner's daughter.

At the top of the stairs, Marge's desk stood as gatekeeper to the rooms and offices behind it. She was cattycorner to a bank of floor-to-ceiling windows looking out at Main Street and beyond.

The elderly secretary gave me a puzzled look, realizing my hands were empty.

"I'm sorry. I forgot them." I'd left the paperwork

unsigned on the kitchen table. "But don't worry. They'll get signed, I assure you."

"I'll have to notarize the last page," Mrs. Kenner said.

"Right."

Thinking our business was done, she beamed at Nikki. "What can I help you with today?"

"Oh, I'm here for moral support." Nikki waved her off.

Mrs. Kenner turned her expectant gaze on me.

"I—" I didn't know how to phrase what I wanted to ask without sounding crazy. "Is Mr. Green in today?"

"He is," she said. "But I'm not sure he's seeing clients. Would you like me to ask?"

I shrugged. "Sure."

Marge stepped over to her desk and buzzed Mr. Green through an intercom.

With Marge's back turned, Nikki's brow furrowed. "What are you doing?" she mouthed.

I shrugged again.

There was something bothering me about Mrs. Kenner and Mr. Green—something I couldn't put my finger on.

Marge handled all of Mr. Green's affairs, including talking to clients like Beau. In the month or so of back and forths with this office before I came down to Florida, I hadn't once spoken to the man himself.

His voice came through the intercom sounding like he was in an echo chamber. "Tell her I have an important phone call this afternoon. But I'd love to speak to her. I can stop by tomorrow morning. Her place."

"He'll do that?" Nikki questioned.

"If he says he'll do it, he'll do it. That's how Artie operates."

"Fine," I agreed.

"Is that all?" Marge asked.

"Just one more thing," I repeated the words I'd heard Columbo say so many times. "Nikki here was wondering about the space beside hers—next to the Grill. Is it still available?"

Nikki opened her mouth to protest and I elbowed her side.

"Oh?" Marge's face lit up "Are y'all thinking to expand? A few more tables would be great on Friday nights."

"And days like today." Nikki shot Marge a fake smile, then narrowed her eyes at me.

"Let's see." Still standing, she leaned over her computer, wheeling an ergonomic mouse like a master. "I don't believe it's sold. Yes. Here it is. Still available. We could take a deposit on it now, if you're ready."

"It might be a touch early for that," Nikki said. "I might should clue Henry in first. You understand."

"Ah, I do. I do. Sometimes it's better if they think it's their idea. If you'd like, I could stop by tomorrow and throw out some subtle hints and mention the space's availability."

"I don't think that'll be necessary. But thank you again for the info." Nikki about-faced and that fake smile turned to a genuine expression of disgust. Her lips tightened. Her jaw set.

She marched away, leaving me standing beside Marge's desk still processing this new information.

Marge inclined her head. "Something else?"

"No one else put down a deposit?" I asked. "You're sure."

"Positive." Marge took her seat. "It's free for the taking. Well, not free. There's the deposit and the lease."

"Sure," I said. "Makes sense."

I did my own about-face, exactly in line with Marge's vantage of downtown Mossy Pointe. I could see Sabal's Grill and across the road to Alaina and Shawna's salon. I could just make out the shed in the alley where Henry was barbecuing. Smoke seeped into the sky above it. Beyond that but obscured, just down the street, was the row of townhomes where Perry had lived.

I remembered the day I got here, driving through town. Marge had seen me. She faced this window; she must surely see everything going on in town. Had she been looking out when Perry was shot? If so, I wondered what she saw.

"Marge…" I spun back to face her again. "Were you here when Perry was murdered? Right here, in your office?"

"I believe I was. Yes."

"Were you looking out this window?"

"Not exactly," she admitted. "But after the gunshot, I was. Who wouldn't be?"

"Can I ask what you saw?"

"Nothing," she said.

"Nothing?" I scowled. "What do you mean nothing?"

"I mean I didn't see anything of value," she said. "At least, not after the shot."

"You saw something before? What was it?"

She straightened. "I'm sure I shouldn't tell you this, but it's already weighing on me. I can't keep it a secret any longer. I saw Beau's work truck. He pulled out and turned south, towing his boat."

That made no sense. If she knew Beau was innocent, why would she want him to take that plea deal?

The answer was so obvious. Beau was covering for someone—*they* were covering for someone.

But why?

I thought about everything I knew.

Perry was fixing cars on the side. Alaina had sold her car —it's why she was riding with Shawna that day at the parlor and why she was riding with her momma to see Beau.

Alaina needed money for something. She'd lied to me about putting a deposit on the space next door to Sabal's. She'd never put down a deposit.

The final piece of the puzzle slid into place. I'd been so keen to look at Ingrid's file, I'd only glanced at Beau's supposed ledger. But it hadn't been written in Beau's untidy scrawl. It had been someone else's handwriting—handwriting I knew well from notes and cootie catchers and MASH.

The ledger had been Alaina's.

She was the bookie. She was the person who owed Perry that money.

And she was his killer. I was sure of it.

"WHAT WAS THAT ALL ABOUT?" Nikki was waiting at the foot of the stairs.

I tried to explain it to her without mentioning any details about Ingrid.

"I don't get it. So, she owed Perry money. Why kill him? They were friends."

"She owed him a lot of money. And I think maybe they had a secret." I didn't elaborate. But maybe, just maybe, Perry knew about Ingrid. Maybe he even helped bury Ingrid's body.

It was the missing piece of the puzzle and something that could only be put together today.

"What kind of secret?" she asked.

"Just a secret." I shrugged.

Nikki pursed her lips in thought, already on to the next thing. "Well, what I really don't get," she continued, "is why Beau would take the rap for her."

"It's Beau," I said. "He was always like that with her—protecting her. Especially after his dad died. You remember."

"I guess. But squabbles at school are in a whole other league—a minor league. We're talking about murder here."

"I know. It's crazy. But believe me, people do crazier things for loved ones."

"We can't let her get away with this," Nikki said. "She has to confess. You're with me on this, right?"

"I am. I agree."

"Good. Let's go get Henry and talk to her."

"Now, I don't think that's a good idea. We should wait for Josh."

"Where is he?" We were halfway to Sabal's Grill, and Nikki picked up the pace.

"Busy," I said.

"Let's just get Henry. It'll be fine. She's not going to kill all three of us. And she has an appointment."

"She also has a gun. We know that much."

"Nah." Nikki shook her head. "Surely, she's ditched that by now."

I couldn't agree with her. The gun might've been hidden at some time, but it wasn't anymore. I couldn't be certain that I hadn't just moved the site of the shooting from Cora's to the salon or the restaurant.

"That's probably not true," I groused.

"Why not?"

"It's complicated." Again, I wanted to tell Nikki how I knew things. But she wouldn't understand.

I couldn't tell her about a fire that had never happened. It struck me that the fire had been because of the gun. It was probably hidden in the firewood beside the shed.

Even if the police had used dogs to search the area for

evidence, they'd have thought they were hitting on the barbecue smell. It was a genius hiding spot.

Alaina had probably retrieved it that morning. Henry would've caught her in the act had I not stormed into the restaurant when I did.

The good thing was, she hadn't used it in that version of events. She'd clocked him with it, started a fire, and left him for dead. But she hadn't used the gun.

"Come on, Willow," Nikki said. "You're an officer of the law. You don't have your weapon?"

"No. I didn't bring it. I didn't think I'd need it here."

"But you're trained for situations like this. Come on. Let's get Henry and go talk to her. She probably feels awful about all of this. She just needs some encouragement to do the right thing." She held the door of the restaurant open. "It's not like she'll have it in her hands. Some scissors, maybe. So, watch out for them."

I nodded. "Fine. Get Henry. I'll watch her hands and keep her away from her purse—and that's before we even say a word. Capisce?"

"Capisce." She darted through the doors to the kitchen, summoning Henry without telling him why.

Confused and flustered, he stormed out, wiping his hands on his apron. "What's this about, Willow?"

"It's best we explain on the fly." Nikki glanced both ways, then raced across the street.

I crossed in much the same fashion, but Henry took his time. We were already through the door of the salon when he called after us, "Hold up a second."

Nikki was undeterred. "Alaina King," she said. "You've got some explaining to do."

"Nikki!" I hissed. "That wasn't the plan."

"Y'all had a plan?" Henry huffed, entering the shop behind us.

Startled, Alaina held her scissors close to her chest. Marcy Chase was equally surprised, her hair in mid trim.

"What's this all about?" the older woman asked.

"It's—it's nothing." Alaina set down the scissors.

I was keeping an eye on her hands while simultaneously scanning the shop for her purse. I couldn't find it.

"And it's not what you three think," she said.

"To be fair," Henry chimed in, "I don't have any clue what this is about."

"Hush it," Nikki scolded. "Let her speak."

"I—I didn't do it."

"Didn't do what?" Henry asked.

Nikki and Marcy shushed him.

But I cut in. "That space over there is still for sale. No one's put a deposit on it. You lied to me."

"It was a white lie, Willow. I really do want to buy that space. At one point, I even had the money for it. But we had a bad few months here. Nikki, you know how owning a business goes—it was like someone was siphoning the salon's money."

"That's not your only money problem," I said. "We know everything. You're the bookie. Where's this other money going—that loan from your mom? Why do you need it?"

She shook her head grimly. "You're right. Beau was never a bookie. That was *my* side hustle. And when Momma caught wind of it, he took the blame. I told him I'd quit."

"Did you?"

"For a little while. Then I took a bet, and I got in deep."

"How?" Henry asked. "I thought bookies always made money?"

"I took too much money on the wrong games. I should've quit while I was ahead."

"Let me guess. Perry was involved in this?"

"That's the thing. Perry was always making small bets, and he always lost. He came to me a few weeks before he died with a lot of money, a whole lot. I gave him good odds. Too good."

"And he won." It wasn't a question.

She nodded.

"When I told Beau, he was furious. I owed him so much money, I sold my car. It wasn't enough. And Beau—you know him—he tried to be a good brother. He was helping *me* that day on the river."

"He took that job for the Swamp Ghosts because of you?"

She nodded.

"Okay," I said. "He was helping you. I get that. What I don't get is why you still need money. If Perry isn't here, isn't that debt erased?"

"That debt is," she said. "But Beau was supposed to do more than one run. Now, the Ghosts say we owe them their money back. Plus interest."

"That's not fair," Nikki said.

"You're right. But it's the price you pay for being stupid."

"I want to help you," I said. "But I need to know. Did you kill Perry?"

"Of course not." She started to cry. "It's just Beau thinks I did. That's why I had to talk to him the other day. He thinks he's in there doing me a favor. But I didn't do it. I don't know who did."

Henry scratched his stubble. "Do we think these Swamp Ghosts had something going on with Perry? Maybe they killed him."

Alaina shook her head. "I don't think so. Perry would've said something. He didn't really have a filter."

"That's true enough," Henry agreed. "He didn't happen to mention where he got all that money, did he?"

"He said it was from fixing cars. Not that I was buying that. But he wouldn't tell me anything else."

"Well, it wasn't from fixing our cars," Henry scoffed.

"I always took mine to Mac," Alaina said.

Dejected, Nikki's shoulders slumped. "So, we still don't know who killed Perry."

"I'm sorry it's not as simple as you thought," Alaina said. "But it wasn't me. And I know it wasn't Beau either."

"I'm glad it wasn't either of you," Nikki said. "I just wish we knew who it was—because your brother's still in jail. And we've run out of suspects."

23

I returned to 2002 Main Street alone.

We were missing something. It had that tip of the tongue sensation, like I knew everything there was to know about the case but the name of the killer still eluded me.

Nikki and Henry—and even Alaina—were operating on half the evidence. They didn't know about Ingrid. It factored in somehow.

My assumption—and I know about assumptions—was that Perry had worked on the vehicle responsible. Perhaps he even knew what happened. Perhaps he was there when it happened.

But that still didn't explain the money he'd bet with Alaina. Or why he got killed.

"You're almost there," Aunt Cora said. "I can tell. Those lines in your forehead will set like that if you're not careful."

"Thanks for the encouragement." I pinched the bridge of my nose. "If it helps, I did what you said, and I'm still not there. I sleuthed, but I'm not good enough."

"Maybe now it's time to use all of your abilities. You put

them all together and you'll make an amazing detective. I'm sure of it."

"Are you suggesting I scry again?"

"I'm suggesting you open yourself up to the possibility that your whole self—the self including your eternal spirit —is far more perceptive and intuitive when whole. If you tap into it, there's nothing that can stop you, dear."

I let her words hang in the air. I let them marinate.

"Ingrid's still gone," I said.

"She'll be back when she's ready."

"I'm afraid that whatever I do, something bad is going to happen."

"The future is always changing, and it's always the same. You can run from your destiny. So many do. You've been running for a long time. But it's those who embrace their destiny who find the future they seek."

"I'll do it," I said.

"You'll do what?"

"I'll try to scry."

"You'll scry," she corrected. "Let's agree never to use that phrase again."

"I was hoping for a Yoda quote or something."

"You won't get it from me," she said.

"I know. It's just you were getting all philosophical there for a second."

I filled a pitcher of water and poured it into the scrying bowl, then got into position. The water was more reflective with the sunlight streaming in through the windows.

Eye to eye with my mirror self, my face blurred away. I found myself again in that void space until I stepped away from my body and the room came back into view.

I went back to my body, just to check that I could.

Going back, I discovered something. That black void

wasn't a void—not entirely. There were thin lines stretching ahead of me, wisps of smoke, like threads.

Behind me was another thread, more solid. When I reached for it, it was like touching a memory.

The world pitched directly into the past, a few hours before, with Josh. I yanked my hand away and the void rushed in around me.

I tried again, reaching further back in my history, this time finding my soul in the road outside with Shawna's Charger barreling through me.

The bumper was a different shade of red.

I jerked my hand away again, too hard this time. Instead of the void, I was in the bedroom again, outside my body.

But I couldn't return. Something was pulling me away.

It forced me through the wall and outside the house. This wasn't like the wind. Not like the wind at all. It was like I was being sucked by a vacuum cleaner. Like a tractor beam had me in its grips. It was pulling me in the direction of Ox Tail Road. Past Sabal's Grill, and past Perry's townhouse.

There was a Dodge Challenger parked in the driveway. In the open garage, I saw an all-too-familiar Crown Victoria.

My spirit form passed through the cars, through the wall, and into Scarlett Myst's living room.

The lights were off. Candles lit. Drapes pulled over the windows. Not a single ray of light penetrated the interior of the townhome.

Scarlett's dining room table was transformed. A beaded tablecloth hid the table. Five crystals were positioned at equal distances from each other on the table. In the center of the invisible pentagon, a tall candle was burning.

Shawna and Scarlett knelt on opposite sides of the table. Their palms were flat against the table, close to each other's hands but not touching. There was a handbell next to Scarlett's right hand.

A seance?

"Spirits, we call to you," Scarlett intoned. "Spirits, we ask you to join us. Speak to us. Link with us. We are your audience, your companions, and your guides. We wish to help you—help you cross over to the other side. That is, if you let us..."

"Are you there, spirit?" Shawna asked, her voice hoarse and dry.

"Someone is," Scarlett answered.

"Who is it?"

I hovered at the edge of the table. Scarlett's eyes bored through me.

"They aren't revealing themselves to me," she said. "All I see is a shadow. Spirit, would you like to speak? Do you need a guide?"

I shook my head.

"What did it say?"

"Nothing," Scarlett spat. "It said nothing."

"Spirit," Shawna pleaded. "Spirit, please. Please—just tell me what I'm supposed to do next. I've done everything you asked me to. Or I've tried to."

Scarlett flung her head back, her palms still pressed on the table. "Spirit, I command you. Speak your truths!"

That tractor beam feeling gripped me tighter, drawing me closer to them. I rebelled against it, and somehow, I came free as another spirit whooshed past me and into Scarlett's body.

The psychic stiffened.

"I am here now," Scarlett said in a husky voice. "And I see I'm not alone."

It was no longer Scarlett's eyes upon me. Someone else had control of her body.

I wanted to slip away, get away, but again, I felt tied to the spot, unable to move my spirit form even an inch.

"Who are you?" it asked me.

I didn't answer.

"Perry?" Shawna croaked. "Is that you again?"

"It's me," he said. "I still have unfinished business. Your debt to me has yet to be paid."

"I... I know. I was just hoping—"

"Hoping?" Scarlett laughed wickedly. Or he did—Perry. "You don't understand hope or know what it's like to have none. Who is this with me? Who did you call here?"

"No one. We called for you. I swear. I don't know who it is."

"Who are you, spirit? Answer me!"

Something compelled me to answer. It bubbled in my nonexistent throat. But I held on to it like bile in a stomach, forcing the words down.

"What do you want from me this time?" Shawna asked.

"I want you to feel my pain," he said. "I want you to know what it's like to lose everything. I want you to see your life flash before your eyes like I did. Like that girl on the road probably did when you hit her. And I want to know who's here with me."

Shawna whimpered. I connected several dots.

"It was you," I whispered.

I wasn't sure which person I was accusing exactly, Shawna or Perry.

Shawna tensed, although I wasn't sure she could hear me.

It was easy to see the difference in Scarlett's features—changes brought on by Perry. He'd heard my accusation.

"I know that voice," he said. "But where do I know it from?"

"What voice?" Shawna trembled. Her eyes darted around the room, glancing off me. "Show yourself. Reveal yourself."

I directed my focus to her and said, "No."

"Who said that?" She started to cry.

Her hands still on the table, nevertheless Scarlett's forearms shook with rage. She yelled—Perry yelled, "Reveal yourself."

The dogs in the other room began to bark.

I fought the sensation, a feeling like I was being ripped out of my skin. I had no skin. But my hands and feet began to glow.

With as much mental fortitude as I could muster, I fought it, and the glowing faded away.

Scarlett slumped over, her eyes shut. I thought I'd won.

Then the shadowy silhouette of a tall, thin man coalesced out of nothing beside her.

His features never formed completely. They were a blur, misshapen when he moved as if parts of him wanted to stay where they were. They reluctantly followed each movement, streaks of shadow dissolving and reforming.

He came closer. And closer. He could move, and I still couldn't.

Perry stopped just inches from me, studying my dull features. He tried to sweep his hand through my chest but his hand melted away with the movement. He tried again with the same result.

"I cannot touch you, whoever you are."

Shawna was crying at the table, bewildered and scared.

"Can I go now?" she asked the slumped over psychic. "Can I please go? Are you still here?"

"Who are you?" Perry sneered. "What business do you have with me?"

I couldn't hold my metaphorical—or metaphysical—tongue any longer. "You know me. I am Willow Brown, a psychic. And I have questions for you. Who are you—who are you to linger here—to make demands of the world when you're no longer a part of it? This is my business because you made it my business, Perry Robinson."

Frightened, Perry recoiled, zooming into Scarlett's body once more.

"It's Willow," the spirit commanding Scarlett barked. "She's here. And she knows what you did."

Shawna's eyes went wide. "No. She can't."

Shawna jerked away from the table, breaking her connection with the psychic. It was like a release button. Suddenly, I could move again.

I zipped across the room and through the wall.

Again, I saw the Dodge Charger. Its bumper, an off shade of red, not quite matching the rest of the car.

I should've paid more attention. I should've known.

Shawna was out the door fast. She had a look of pure determination on her face, her eyes set in the direction of Aunt Cora's parlor.

At the speed of thought, I was home. I scrambled, looking for my phone. I had to call Josh. He had to get here before those shots were fired.

Shawna's car wasn't far behind me. In less than a minute, she was there at the door. The unlocked door.

I reached the purple phone in the parlor. I dialed the rotary nine just before she burst through the door, a gun in hand.

"Willow, we need to talk," she said. "We can work this all out."

"There's nothing to work out," I said.

"There is. There's plenty to work out. You don't have any proof. There is no proof except what I've got in my hands. And I'll do a better job of hiding it this time."

"You mean it won't be in the firewood outside Sabal's?" I asked her.

"Hang up the phone," she commanded.

The phone crashed down on the cradle. I held up my empty hands.

Shawna's hands were trembling around the grip of the gun. She ordered me to get down on my knees.

This was it. The end—the end I'd been expecting since I was seven years old. My vision fully realized.

Shawna's red fingernails came in and out of focus. As did the barrel of the gun. It was a small thing, a snub-nosed revolver. Small enough she could carry it around in her purse.

How can such a small thing be so deadly?

Her finger hovered near the trigger. Those nails again, blood red.

"So, you've figured it out?"

"Not quite," I said.

"I knew you'd be trouble," she said. "I knew it. Coming back here was a mistake."

"I see that now."

"I wanted to believe you—that you were telling us the truth. But you do have the gift. Don't you? There's no use lying to me now, is there?"

"I have a gift," I conceded. "Not *the* gift. I'm not like Aunt Cora."

She nodded her head, her arms flexing with the movement. I flinched but nothing happened.

"You're right," Shawna said. "You're not like Cora. You're

nowhere near as good as she was. I had to be smart. I never came here again after it happened. She would've known— seen it in the cards or on my face. I don't know. Something would've tipped her off that I killed that girl. By the way, how did you figure it out?"

"Your car," I said. "The bumper's been fixed. Perry did that shoddy work. Not Mac."

"How silly," Shawna said. "And how did the body get found? I'm guessing that was you too. It's already on *Neighbor Sleuths*."

"I can see her—could see her. I could talk to her too. Her name was Ingrid."

"Funny. She spoke to you and not me, her killer. Not Perry—no, he haunted me."

"What happened? Why'd you kill Ingrid?"

"Stop saying her name! I never wanted to know who she was. The only thing I wanted to know was why she was walking on the side of the road that night."

Shawna lowered the gun as if her shoulders were aching from holding it there so long. When she did, I rocked out of the way, but she found me with it again. She got close. Real close. The background faded. I knew this part of the vision well.

"I'd been drinking," she said. "Not much. But enough. I shouldn't've been driving. Honestly, I thought she was a deer. When I got out of the car and saw her, I panicked."

"You buried her?" I asked. "By yourself?"

"I called Perry," she admitted. "He needed money—he always needed money."

I had to keep her talking. I had to find a way out of this. My visions didn't always play out like they did in my head, not if I intervened.

And there was still time to intervene.

"Yes. He fixed the bumper—just like you thought."

"Then what?"

"What do you think?" she asked coldly. "He got himself in a pickle. He asked for more money. I gave it to him. Then he got himself in another. Never let a gambler blackmail you. They'll bleed you dry—which is exactly what he did. I drained my savings. Then I took money from the salon."

Now I knew where Alaina's money went and where Perry's money came from.

"It never was enough," she went on. "He was always wanting more. He even said I should get a loan from the bank."

"So you shot him?"

"He got what he deserved!"

"And they never looked at you for it?"

She shook her head. "Not really. Besides, I was with Alaina at the salon—at least, I was according to her. You know how forgetful she can be. Ask her at lunchtime what she ate for breakfast—she won't remember. So, when they checked my story, she agreed with it."

"Is that what you think's going to happen now? When they find my body, is she just going to agree y'all were together?"

"I'll think of something. I always do."

Stall. Stall. Stall.

"Do you remember my dream?" I asked her, peering around the barrel of the gun. "When we were kids. I told you about it at a slumber party. Do you remember?"

She nodded. "The woman with the red nails and the gun?"

"It turns out that's you," I said.

Her knuckles whitened. "What a crazy coincidence."

"It's not a coincidence. It's real. I helped you. Perry's gone now because I pushed him away."

"Perry was never going to leave me alone. He was going to haunt me the rest of my life. I should thank you for what you did back there."

"Then thank me. Turn yourself in. Ingrid was an accident. Perry was using you. I'm not saying you won't go to prison…"

"None of that will matter. The witnesses are dead. But if you're gone, I can still get away with it."

"If that's really how you think, just get it over with," I said. "If you can kill three people like it's nothing, then get it over with. I'm tired of pleading with you, Shawna. I'll see you in the next life."

"Have it your way."

She squeezed the trigger.

24

The bullet passed straight through my head. It was loud—loud enough to snap my spirit into my real body. My head went straight into the scrying bowl with a splash. I sucked in and sputtered water.

I wasn't dead—not in the way the vision had led me to believe all these years. But I wasn't yet free from it.

Downstairs, Shawna was cussing a blue streak. Seeing a body up and vanish might elicit such a response.

But once the surprise wore off, she'd have been on to me. At least downstairs, in my spirit form, I had some protection. I could steer her elsewhere. Now, I was stuck upstairs with nothing to defend myself against a proven killer—a killer whose attempt to murder me just now had gone completely off script.

Done with obscenities, her footsteps loud and purposeful, she left the parlor. The stairs creaked under her weight, one after another.

"Are you a ghost too, Willow?" Her voice carried up the stairwell. "Was that your secret? Or was that some kind of mind trick?"

I had to come up with a plan. Why did I have to be behind the first door? If I'd only been quieter, she wouldn't have come up the stairs.

"Are you up here, Willow? You remember when we used to play hide and seek? You were never any good. I could always hear you breathing."

I held onto hope that Josh would get here soon. In the vision, his radio dispatcher had called out shots fired. There'd been a single shot so far. I hoped it was enough.

I cracked the door open to watch the end of the hallway and the stairs. There was no use locking it. Just delaying the inevitable.

Shawna held the gun pointed toward the floor. And as she set foot on the second floor, I heard the door at the end of hallway swing open.

The blur of a young woman came flying down the hall from my old room. Ingrid tackled Shawna, and they both went crashing down the stairs.

By the time I got down the stairs, there was just a single body, limp and twisted. Shawna was breathing heavily, but she was breathing.

Carefully, I located the gun and moved it out of her reach. I dialed 911 from the purple phone in the parlor. And about ten seconds later, Josh came bursting through the front door, ready for action, a minute too late.

AN AMBULANCE CAME and took Shawna to the nearest hospital, thirty miles away.

Before anyone else arrived, I had a talk with Josh, who understood the situation better than anyone. We talked about my visions and Ingrid's part in Shawna's demise. He helped smooth out the details in my interviews, first by a detective with the sheriff's department, and finally, by an apologetic Chief Hammonds.

The chief, more than anybody, seemed pleased for Ingrid's story to be resolved. Beau's innocence factored into our conversation. His release would take several days to process. But I had confidence it would happen.

I could leave town knowing I'd done a good thing.

It took hours for the house to clear out.

I was alone. Ingrid was gone. I doubted she'd return. And I hadn't seen the cat since scrying.

I searched the house and found her in the kitchen, doing her own scrying, studying her reflection in the water dish. She lapped some up, then jumped on the table, settling on top of the paperwork.

"You still haven't signed?"

"I'm getting to it."

"Are you though?"

"Stop." I wasn't in the mood for games or riddles. I was exhausted, and I still had a lot left to do here. "I know you want me to stay, but it's not in the cards."

"You haven't consulted the cards," Cora countered.

"Should I?"

The cat bristled. "When you embraced your gifts—"

"But they're not gifts."

"Hush up and listen. When you embraced your gifts—your abilities—you took responsibility for them. It's not something you can take back."

"I don't plan to," I said.

"That's what I wanted to hear." The cat stalked across the table, its tail high. It leaped down, landing gracefully on four paws.

It turned its head, regarding me with cold yellow eyes.

There was a knock on the front door.

I could swear the cat smirked as if Cora had known that knock was coming. "You better get that."

In my head, I listed the people it could be—there were quite a few: Nikki and Henry, Mrs. King and Alaina, or possibly Scarlett Myst. I needed some sort of apology from her too.

"I've come to hate this door," I told Cora. "The police didn't turn the light on, did they?"

She didn't offer a response. Instead, she stalked through the house ahead of me.

"If I were staying, I'd invest in a peephole."

I flipped on the porch light and swung the door open. The muggy night air wafted into the house along with a song of frogs and insects.

It was no one I expected.

A man holding a bouquet of lilies just below his beautiful smile. He didn't seem real.

"Tim?" I whispered. "What on Earth are you doing here?"

25

Tim and I stayed up late that night discussing a lot of things, including the large gray elephant in the room. It wasn't just my investigation and Shawna's attempted murder. I had to tell him the truth: I was a psychic. To which he replied that he knew. He'd always known.

How much he knew was up for debate—another time.

There were other matters. Things like what to do with Cora's house, her cat, and our jobs.

It took a while—and a lot of soul searching of the non-scrying variety—but we came to a consensus. I agreed to hear him out, not because he'd driven down and not because I owed him anything but because I love Timothy Brown.

We settled in ways I'd never have predicted, not even if the vision of them had struck me like a door to the face.

My nose was still sore and slightly swollen. He'd noticed.

The next morning, I let Tim sleep. How he managed it with the sunlight streaming into the room upstairs, I'd never understand.

I went through Cora's cat routine, feeding her canned food and letting her outside while I cooked breakfast.

A little while later, she watched as I rummaged through the parlor. I took stock of what was there—twenty decks of tarot cards, a boatload of crystals, thirty-six candles, three boxes of matches, several spent grill lighters, and so on.

"Let me guess—you're selling my stuff on one of those online auctions?"

She surprised me. "That's not actually the plan. You weren't listening in last night?"

"I started to, but you two are kind of boring when you're getting along. What's this plan entail? Am I moving in with you two in Virginia? Should I pack my bags?"

"I'm not sure I want to tell you what the plan is. Maybe I want you to be surprised."

"I can see the future, dear. I know you're staying."

"Then why be coy about it?"

She hunched her cat shoulders. "I don't know all the details... yet. I thought maybe since you're staying, you should open up. Do a reading or two."

"A reading? Haven't I honed my psychic skills enough for a few days? I could use a break."

"The readings aren't for you. They're for the town, the people—they need to get back to some normalcy."

"More like abnormalcy." I laughed at my joke. "They have Scarlett Myst for readings. I'm going to do something else with this space."

Her interest piqued, the cat scooted closer. She darted away a moment later.

The stairs shook under Tim's weight. He stomped down and stopped outside the parlor. He looked left, then he looked right.

He scowled. "I could swear I heard voices. You talking to yourself again?"

"You know me." I smiled up at him.

"You're right. I do. Knowing you, you're starving right about now. It's almost lunchtime."

"I can always eat," I said sheepishly. "Only I haven't picked up anything from the store."

"I saw a greasy spoon in town, The Majesty Diner."

"Oh, no. We can't go there. We're eating at Sabal's Grill."

"Nikki's place? That's fine too." He held out his arm for me.

I rolled my eyes but humored him. "Tim," I said, "you're sure this is a good idea?"

"We both need a fresh start."

"Agreed. And P.I. licenses."

"Those too," he said. "Brown and Brown, Private Detectives."

"Private and psychic."

"It doesn't have the same ring to it."

"All right—Brown and Brown, it is. But we keep the light in the window."

"The light?" He arched an eyebrow.

"The palm in the window. It means we're open."

He nodded.

Aunt Cora darted through our legs. She took up a position on the ottoman.

"The cat gives me the creeps." Tim shuddered. "I swear she looks at me like she knows what I'm saying."

"You're being paranoid." I playfully elbowed him in the ribs.

"I'm not paranoid. She's doing it right now!"

"Like I said, you're being paranoid." I glowered at Aunt

Cora, who did her little shrug without shoulders thing again.

Tim's hand was on the door when someone knocked on it.

"Who could that be?"

"Any number of people," I said grimly.

Again, I was taken by surprise.

The person outside, I knew by voice and reputation. When I was younger, his face was on billboards around town. There were also commercials with his stern face leveled at a camera saying things like, "If you were caught drinking and driving, don't call me. I only represent the innocent."

Artemis Green had told me he'd swing by, but it had completely slipped my mind.

Sunlight flooded the foyer.

He was even oilier than I remembered, having aged the twenty years less gracefully than a man of his stature should. He had heavy jowls that hung down from his face like a Saint Bernard's. I imagined he had to be careful buttoning his top button and tying his tie.

"Mrs. Brown, I presume? Mrs. Willow Brown?"

"That's me."

"I believe we had an appointment. And I have news. Great news."

"You do?" I inclined my head.

About Beau? Was he already out of jail?

"I found a buyer for this house. And they're offering full price."

"Oh." That was a surprise—especially considering I hadn't set a price.

And we'd just decided to stay. Not that I'd made any

calls, not even to my boss in Creel Creek. It wasn't official yet.

"You've signed the paperwork, haven't you? You told Marge it was ready."

"About that," I said. "I'm not sure—we're not sure we want to sign. We might stay here a while."

"Stay here?

"It's been decided." Tim sounded positive.

Artemis Green pressed his lips together, his pencil-thin mustache bristling. "I don't believe we've met."

"The name's Timothy Brown. And you're right. We haven't had the pleasure."

I cut in. "This is Mr. Green, our lawyer. He was Aunt Cora's lawyer. He wanted to help me sell the house."

"Most people just call me Art or Artie," Mr. Green said.

"Well, Art," Tim tried to sound polite but failed completely, "we decided not to sell the house."

"I heard you. But I've already found a buyer." Mr. Green stepped closer. He put a polished shoe on the threshold. "In fact, this buyer might be willing to go over the asking price. You stand to make a substantial sum from this."

"We're not interested." Tim stood firm.

"You could still stay in Mossy Pointe," Mr. Green said. "There are plenty of homes for sale."

Tim made a face. "Who's this buyer? Why this house? Like you said, there's plenty of *other* places to live. We're staying here."

"Are you?" Mr. Green's eyebrows knitted together. He poked his head in and surveyed what he could see. It wasn't much. And none of it was ours.

"We will be," Tim said. "Isn't that right, Willow?"

"It is," I agreed. "I'm sorry, Mr. Green. We're not interested."

No longer in the mood for a stroll to Sabal's, I tried to shut the door. Mr. Green's foot didn't budge.

"You're making a mistake. This offer's only good through the end of the day."

"Thanks, anyway." Tim slammed the door. He shook his head and muttered, "You're making a big mistake. Damn if I don't hate lawyers. That guy was creepier than the cat. Come on, I'm ready to eat."

We went outside hand in hand. It had been a minute, maybe less, and there was no sign of Artemis Green anywhere. No car. He wasn't walking down the driveway, and he wasn't anywhere in the yard.

"That's strange," Tim said.

"It totally is."

The hairs on my neck prickled as if I'd seen a ghost.

Then it occurred to me—maybe I had.

ACKNOWLEDGMENTS

Thanks to Ellen Campbell who edited this book. To Paula Lester for proofreading. To Jason Gussow for beta reading. To Jenn for being an amazing partner.

And special thanks to my mother, she has a spirit beyond compare.

As always, thanks to my family and friends who help support me. You're the best.

BY CHRISTINE ZANE THOMAS

Witching Hour starring 40 year old witch Constance Campbell

Book 1: Midlife Curses

Book 2: Never Been Hexed

Book 3: Must Love Charms

Book 4: You've Got Spells

Book 5: As Grimoire As It Gets

Book 6: While You Were Spellbound

Witching Hour: Psychics coming early 2021

Book 1: The Scrying Game

Book 2: The Usual Psychics

Tessa Randolph Cozy Mysteries written with Paula Lester

Grim and Bear It

The Scythe's Secrets

Reap What She Sows

Foodie File Mysteries starring Allie Treadwell

The Salty Taste of Murder

A Choice Cocktail of Death

A Juicy Morsel of Jealousy

The Bitter Bite of Betrayal

Comics and Coffee Case Files starring Kirby Jackson and Gambit

ABOUT CHRISTINE ZANE THOMAS

Christine Zane Thomas is the pen name of a husband and wife team. A shared love of mystery and sleuths spurred the creation of their own mysterious writer alter-ego.

While not writing, they can be found in northwest Florida with their two children, their dachshund Queenie, and schnauzer Tinker Bell. When not at home, their love of food takes them all around the South. Sometimes they sprinkle in a trip to Disney World. Food and Wine is their favorite season.

Made in the USA
Monee, IL
07 July 2021

72982750R00121